LOVE LIKE A COWBOY'S SMILE

A Sweet Christian Romance

Seeking Home

CAROLYNE AARSEN

Chapter 1

*M*iriam yanked open the hood of her small black sports car, glared down at the smoking engine, then sneezed as the harsh smell of leaking radiator fluid assaulted her nostrils.

She pushed back her long hair and dragged her hand down the back of her head, rolling her neck to ease the kink in it. She was tired, cranky, and worn out. For the past few days, she'd been putting in twelve hours behind the wheel to get here. It was just her ill luck to break down only three miles from her destination.

With a sigh, she looked around. All she saw were rolling hills and copses of poplar and spruce trees broken by stubbled fields ready for spring planting. Fields she had ridden past for most of her life on her way to school. Fields where she had ridden her horse before spring planting and after combining.

The county of Waylen. Her old home.

She hadn't been back since that horrible day, ten years ago, when she had walked down these very roads, tears blurring her eyes as she headed toward the highway, her possessions thrown together in a knapsack slung over her shoulder. She had never known why leaving abruptly was called "running away." She had walked every dreary and heartsick step on that early summer morning, her boyfriend's words ringing in her ears. Jake didn't love her anymore.

Halfway to town, her mother had caught up with her, and high drama was replaced by her mother's usual carping and nagging.

Miriam sneezed once more, yanked back to the present by the stark reality that there was still no vehicle in sight. She pulled her phone out to call a tow truck and made a face.

No service? Seriously?

Guess she was walking down a gravel road in sandals far more suited to paved city sidewalks.

Coming full circle, she thought, adding a deep sigh.

She pulled out the keys to the car and threw her cell phone in her large handbag along with a bottle of water she always had on hand. She was thankful that her cotton pants were thin. If she got too warm, she could put the cardigan she wore into the bag and risk sunburning her shoulders. She just wished she had a hat.

Shouldering her bag, she took a deep breath and started walking down the road. She pushed aside her irritation, reminding herself that she was on country time now. What would be would be, and fussing wouldn't change anything.

Besides, this was supposed to be a vacation. A time to catch her breath before she went back to try to save her fledgling business the only way she knew how.

Wearing designer clothes, strutting her stuff down a runway, cameras whirring and flashing as she paraded the latest creations of the hottest designer of the moment.

Miriam pulled a face as she skirted a small puddle in the middle of the road. The idea of going back to the hurrying and waiting that characterized most of her modeling career held scant appeal. But if that's what she had to do, she would do it.

The sun shone down on her unprotected head, and not for

the first time since she'd pointed her little car west did Miriam wonder why she hadn't sold the family farm in western Alberta from the safety of New York.

As long as her mother, Edna, had been alive, the farm had remained unsold. It was where Edna had been born. Even after Edna moved to Toronto, she made it quite clear the farm was not to be sold while she was still alive.

Now her mother was dead. Miriam needed the money to cover part of the debt she had amassed when a supplier defaulted on a delivery but still took her money which had created a spiral she couldn't claw her way out of.

So, to try to pay down the debt, she fell back on the one thing she knew. Modeling. She found a new agent. A good man and sincere Christian. Carl Hanson. It was Carl who had suggested she go home between jobs. Take a driving holiday.

But, he had warned her, *make sure you're back in time for the big job I pulled a lot of strings to get you.*

Runway work for the hottest new designer with options for a lot more work if she proved herself.

"Drive back to your farm," Carl had advised her when she just about cried on his shoulder, the stress wearing her down. "Don't sell it from here. Go back to your past. Catch your breath. Take a break from your trouble. Make a clean break with your past and move on."

"If Carl could only see me now," she muttered, adjusting her bag on her shoulder.

She had gone only a quarter of a mile, and her feet were already sore, when the growl of an engine made her turn. But she saw nothing behind her.

Heat shimmered up from the gravel road, and below her, the land flowed away. Her eyes followed the brown hills, broken by groupings of poplar and spruce. The bare, lacy branches of the aspen trees held a hint of soft green that would be full when it was time for her to leave again.

These rolling hills had occupied her mind many times, even in the most exotic of locales.

A yearning caught her unaware, reminding her of past events, still unresolved. Events that Carl knew occupied her mind. Events he had hinted that she should try to settle before she came back to a busy and time-consuming schedule.

Miriam stopped, her heart lifting at the sound of a vehicle coming closer.

She heard it slow down, probably by her car, then speed up again. A cloud of dust roiled behind it as it topped the rise.

The sun reflected off the glass of the cab, so she couldn't see the driver. The truck skidded to a halt on the loose gravel, and the driver opened his door and got out.

She put on her most polite "I'm sorry to bother you" smile, as the man came closer and stopped in front of her, wiping his hands on his blue jeans, his white T-shirt already stained with grease and dirt.

Dark brown hair in need of a cut fell across his forehead. Heavily lashed brown eyes stared at her from beneath level brows. His strong jaw was dark with stubble.

Miriam acknowledged his good looks almost analytically. Her job as a model put her in the company of many handsome men, but this man had an earthy appeal that spoke more strongly to her than did the clean, stylized looks she was used to. She was about to raise her hand to shake his when recognition dawned, and her stomach plunged.

Of all the people she would have to meet under these circumstances! Jake Steele. Next-door neighbor, one-time boyfriend, and the man over whom she had shed a thousand tears.

She swallowed, her mouth suddenly dry, as she realized he didn't recognize her.

"I'm guessing that was your car parked back there. Do you need some help?" Jake asked, his deep voice quiet. He looked down at her, his weight resting on one leg, his one thumb hooked on the belt loop of his jeans. The dusty white T-shirt and the faded jeans enhanced his masculine appeal. It wasn't lost on Miriam.

A girl can still lose herself in his eyes, she thought, remembering another time on this same road when she had done just that. When she and Jake had sat on the tailgate of his pickup, arms around each other, ignoring the moonlit landscape below them, lost in each other and the wonder of their love. A love Miriam had promised Jake would be his forever.

A love he had quickly replaced—with her best friend.

What a fool she had been then!

And despite the time between then and now, anger boiled up.

The intensity surprised her. Also, the fact that after ten years and many disappointments, she had any emotions to spare for this man.

Taking a breath, she controlled herself. She hadn't come here to get even, just to find closure.

"My car broke down. I'm pretty sure it's the radiator. I was wondering if you could help me out."

Jake scratched his head, frowning, as if trying to place her. "Were you headed to my folks' farm? There's no other place down this road."

Miriam swallowed down the unexpected hurt at his lack of recognition, shifting her purse on her shoulder. "You don't know who I am, do you?"

Jake shrugged, the casual movement giving her a fresh pain. Once upon a time, years ago, she could have come up with some smart comment that would have made him smile, that would have eased away her own awkwardness. But life had been difficult the past few years, and laughter and joking didn't come as readily.

Instead, she looked directly at him and simply said, "I'm Miriam."

She could tell from his expression the moment he finally

recognized her. "Miriam Spencer?" he asked, his eyes narrowing.

Miriam made herself hold his gaze without blinking. "Not too many other Miriams around Waylen," she said, forcing herself to match his own even tone.

He frowned, his hands now hanging loosely at his sides as he continued to look at her.

A soft spring breeze swirled around them, and the sharp trill of a red-tailed hawk shivered down. Anticipation hovered around them.

How many times had she relived this reunion in her mind? How many times had she imagined herself coming back, full of self-confidence, preferably on the arm of an equally self-confident and attractive man?

Miriam Spencer returning to the place of her humiliation.

Miriam Spencer, in control of her life and her destiny.

"We've been hearing a lot about you," was all he finally said, his voice cool.

Miriam stiffened in reaction to his sudden reserve. She saw the condemnation in his eyes, felt the censure. She wondered which of the many false stories written about her in the tabloids he believed.

"I'm sure you have." She tilted her head, lifted her chin, and held his gaze. "But you should know you can't believe everything you read." She turned to go, but Jake caught her by the arm, turning her back.

"I'm sorry," he said automatically, but she could see his apology lacked conviction. He was merely being polite. The way he always was. "Did you call a tow truck?"

"No. There's no service here."

"Right. I keep forgetting. So, do you need a lift to your place so you can call from there? Or I could give you a tow myself."

"That's okay. I don't want to put you out." Miriam shifted her bag, wishing she could just leave, but Jake still had his hand on her arm. Try as she might, she couldn't ignore the strength and warmth of it through her shirt. "And you can let go of my arm," she said, looking down pointedly.

Jake dropped his hand as if her arm were on fire. "Sorry," he muttered. Then he looked at her. "Look, it's a long walk back." He glanced down at the thin sandals on her feet, her loose-fitting linen pants that were already stained with dust from the road. "My truck is no limo, but it will get you to your place quicker than walking."

Miriam wished she could say no. She didn't want his help. But a three-mile walk, in the sandals he had looked at so disdainfully, wasn't appealing. Accepting his offer was the mature thing to do. And that was part of the reason for this trip, wasn't it? To show herself that she had gotten past this part of her life?

So, she nodded. "Thanks for the offer," she said, and she walked around to the passenger side of the truck.

He followed, saying nothing, and just as she was about to open the door, he reached past and did it for her.

Miriam nodded her thanks, then climbed up into the truck and settled on the seat.

Jake got in without saying a word, put the truck into gear, and they were off. A song blared from the radio, but Jake reached over and switched it off. Miriam wished he hadn't. The muted roar of the truck, the faint whiff of diesel mixed with dust that permeated the cab—both combined to bring back surprisingly sharp memories.

Memories of being scrunched awkwardly into a narrow tractor cab, riding along with Jake while he plowed, cultivated, seeded, sprayed, swathed, or combined, singing along with songs on the radio, as they looked into each other's eyes. It didn't matter what job he had to do on his foster father's farm, she usually managed to finagle a ride with him.

Now, as then, Miriam couldn't help but glance over at

Jake. His dark hair still curled over the back of his collar, still invited a girl to run her hands through it.

Give your head a shake, Miriam chided herself, sighing lightly. He's married, and even if he wasn't, you're not looking, remember?

She blamed her lapse on the surroundings. It was as if driving down these roads, seeing an endless sky, cirrus clouds sweeping across its blue bowl, had immediately erased the past ten years in one quick swipe. It was as if being back here turned her from a woman, determined to keep her heart to herself, back into that young girl who gave it to the first boy she had been attracted to. Jake Steele.

Stick to the plan, she reminded herself. *You're here to sell the farm, to put the past to rest. Then you go back east and keep struggling.*

Miriam pushed the depressing thoughts aside and forced herself to ignore Jake, to look around. The road followed a ridge that cut alongside a hill rising above them on one side and flowing away from them on the other. Rock Lake was at the bottom of the hill, hidden by a large stand of spruce and aspen tinged with the pale green of new growth.

Ahead of them lay more fields, more bushes, alternating shade and warmth as they drove along. Not much had changed since she left, she realized. The trees looked the same, the fields were the same.

It was like stepping back in time, and she shivered in reaction.

"Too cold?" Jake asked, finally speaking. He didn't wait for her answer but reached over to adjust the air-conditioning.

"Thanks." She fidgeted on the seat, the silence in the cab pressing down on her. "How's the weather been?" she blurted out, and then forced herself not to groan. What a cliché question. He would think she was a total airhead.

"Good."

"Seeding done?"

"Not yet."

"How much land do you farm now?"

Jake shrugged. "About eight quarters."

"Do you still have the cows?"

"Yup."

"How many?"

"One hundred head. Just commercial."

"Wow. You and Fred have expanded."

Jake only nodded, and Miriam turned away in exasperation. He wasn't going to make this one bit easy for her. As if he had the right to be so taciturn.

Miriam wished she had never accepted his offer of a ride. Wished she had just kept walking. Sore feet and overheating would have been preferable to this heavy atmosphere.

But she was a big girl now and determined to see this through. After all, he and Paula lived half a mile from her farm; she would be seeing them over the course of her stay. Better to try to get some of that first-time awkwardness out of the way before she met Paula, her old friend—Jake's wife.

"So, how is Paula?" she asked, pleased at the even tone in her voice. A tone that didn't betray the hurt that gripped her even now.

Jake's hands tightened on the steering wheel, and he threw her a quick glance, then looked away. "You've really been out of touch, haven't you?" he asked, his voice dangerously quiet.

Miriam almost pressed herself back against the seat at the anger in his voice. "I don't understand what you're talking about," she said sharply. What right did he have to use that tone with her? He was the one who had gotten married barely four months after she left. She knew she had been out of touch, but what did she have to say to either him or her old friend?

Jake stared straight ahead, his expression grim. "Paula died three years ago." His words were clipped, his voice devoid of emotion.

Miriam stared at him, her hands numb, an icy cold gripping her temples as she tried to make sense of what he had said.

"What—Paula...dead?" She struggled to find the right words, to find some meaning in what he said. Why didn't she know this? How come no one had told her?

Because you pulled away from Waylen and anything to do with anyone here.

"She rolled her car on a gravel road and wasn't wearing her seat belt. The doctor told us she died right away." Jake looked up again, his lips thin. "I'm guessing this is a shock for you?"

Miriam shook her head, still struggling over what to ask, what to say, looking at him as if to find answers to the questions. "I didn't know," she said weakly. She pulled her hand over her face and then bit her lip as disbelief fled and sadness welled up. After all, Paula had been her friend, even though Miriam had not contacted her once she found out about Paula and Jake's marriage.

Miriam swallowed the sorrow, a belated sense of guilt washing over her.

"I'm so sorry, Jake. This must be difficult for you." The words were inadequate, but protocol deemed they be spoken. "I'm sure it's been hard for Fred and Tilly, as well," Miriam continued quietly.

"Mom and Dad had a really hard time with it." His words were quietly spoken, and the silence of before settled once again between them.

"And how are Fred and Tilly?"

"Okay." Jake hesitated, as if to show her she didn't deserve to hear anything about his foster parents, the same people who had been second parents to Miriam, as well. "Dad had a heart attack a month ago. The doctor said he sustained a lot of damage, so he's still pretty weak."

Miriam wanted to say that she was sorry. Again. How much apologizing was she going to be doing on this trip?

"I hope he gets better."

"So do I," Jake said heavily.

In those three words, Miriam clearly heard the love she knew Jake held for his foster parents. Though he had moved to Fred and Tilly's place as a teenager, he had become like their own son. He saw them as his parents.

Miriam swallowed again, staring straight ahead, battling the envy she felt. Jake, who once had nothing, now had everything—a family of his own, parents who loved him, a direction to his life.

Whereas she, who had once had it all...

The rest of the drive continued in silence, but now other emotions had been added to the mix, creating a tension in Miriam that built with each roll of the truck's wheels.

She was thankful when she saw Fred and Tilly's driveway, the same brightly painted horse-drawn plow at the end of it.

Jake turned in, and anticipation mixed with dread washed through her.

"I'll just let Tilly and Fred know what's going on, and then I can take you to your place," he said, his words breaking the long silence. "You may as well come in and say hello."

Miriam only nodded, clutching her purse as her own heartbeat sped up. Her apprehension was a combination of nerves and fear and another kind of guilt at the thought of meeting Fred and Tilly again. As a young girl, she had spent many hours sitting at their kitchen table, had followed Fred around while he did his chores.

Miriam's father had died when she was ten, and Edna had had to work in town. Saturdays found Miriam either helping Tilly in the kitchen or working alongside Fred—feeding cows, helping with the calves, or helping with any of the myriad repairs required on the farm. The Prins's home became her second home, a haven from Edna's constant criticism and "big plans" for her daughter.

Miriam had had no big plans. All she had ever wanted was to stay in Waylen.

When she was thirteen, a social worker had brought Jake to Fred and Tilly's, and her plans changed to include marrying Jake.

When she first saw the dangerously good-looking teenager, she knew in her heart that she loved only him. Her mother, of course, made sure Miriam knew *her* opinion. "A foster child from who knows where." Miriam could still hear her harsh, berating voice. "You stay away from him, Miriam. Boy like him is nothing but trouble," Edna had said, contempt ringing in her voice.

Miriam had laughed at the notion. A girl who had been teased most of her school years for being skinny could hardly net the attention of someone like Jake.

But to her amazement, she had. Even Paula—beautiful, dark-haired, and curvaceous Paula—could hardly believe that Jake would prefer Miriam to her.

But he had. At least at first, Miriam reminded herself.

Miriam closed her eyes at a sudden surge of pain and sorrow. Paula, her one-time friend. Dead. She could hardly bear thinking about it.

Jake parked the truck and, without giving Miriam a second glance, got out. Miriam swallowed, rubbing her damp hands over her pants. What would she say to Fred, to Tilly? she thought, hesitating. Too much time had elapsed, and she had done nothing to bridge that gap.

Well, she was here now. She had to start this homecoming sooner or later. She slung her bag over her shoulder and climbed out of the truck.

"Thanks for the ride and the help," she said to Jake, lifting her head to look confidently up at him.

"You're welcome."

He stood back, allowing her to go first.

They had just made it to the cement sidewalk by the house when the door burst open.

"Daddy, Daddy, you're home." A little girl, her braids flying out behind her, came running up to Jake and launched herself at him. Miriam felt a lump in her throat.

A little girl. Jake had a little girl.

Jake caught the girl, swung her around. For the first time since Miriam had seen him, she noticed a heartfelt and sincere smile on his face.

"Hey, Pipper," he said, hugging his daughter tightly. He straightened, holding the little girl on one arm. Her arms were wrapped around his neck, and as they turned to Miriam, she felt a harsh clutch of jealousy. She could see Jake in the deep brown of the little girl's eyes, Jake in the thick waves of her hair—but Paula in the coy smile.

"Hi," the girl said. "My name is Taryn. What's yours?"

"This is Miriam," Jake interjected, settling Taryn on his arm. "Her car broke down on the road, and I gave her a ride here."

Taryn nodded, staring at Miriam as if studying her. "Has she been here before?"

"Not since you were born." Jake turned to Miriam. "Why don't you come in a minute? I'm sure Mom and Dad would like to see you."

Miriam nodded, feeling very much the outsider. Taryn continued to stare at her, and Miriam couldn't keep her eyes off Jake's daughter.

She looked so much like her father, it made her heart hurt.

Miriam followed Jake up the walk, suddenly hesitant at the thought of meeting Tilly and Fred again. Guilt and shame vied with one another as her steps followed the old familiar pathway. She had skipped up this walk as a young girl. She had run up it as a teenager. She had always come here with a happy heart, the feeling that someone who cared for her lived here. This had been a home.

Jake pushed the screen door open and set Taryn down on the floor. "Take your socks off, missy," he said. "They're all dirty."

Taryn dropped down and, lifting her foot, yanked off the once-white sock. "I was waiting for you," she said, grinning up at him. "You didn't have supper."

Miriam dropped her bag on the chair in the porch that had always been there, without even realizing what she was doing. She had to catch herself before she kicked off her sandals and ran past Jake up the steps to sit at the kitchen table. This porch was so familiar.

But the presence of a much older Jake and his daughter showed her all too clearly how much had changed.

Taryn got up, still looking at Miriam with a puzzled expression. "Did you know my mommy?" she asked.

Jake turned to his daughter, his surprise evident. "What did you say?" he asked her.

Taryn turned to him, still frowning. "I saw her picture in my mommy's book."

"What book?"

"The one with that Miriam lady's pictures in it."

"Is that you, Jake?" Tilly called from the kitchen, interrupting the puzzling moment. She came to the door, wiping her hands on a towel, smiling at her son. "How was your day, dear?"

Miriam's throat tightened at the sight of Tilly. The woman's face held a few more lines; her short, straight hair was now completely gray. But she wore the same glasses she had worn ten years ago, and the soft blue eyes were unchanged, the warm smile still welcoming.

"Good," Jake said succinctly. "I brought someone back." He stepped aside, gesturing toward Miriam.

Tilly lifted her hand up to readjust her glasses, and she squinted at Miriam, who tried not to fidget. "My goodness," Tilly said as she recognized who it was, her lined face breaking out into a large smile, her arms opening. "Miriam? Little Miriam Spencer?"

Tilly walked past Jake straight to Miriam, and enfolded her in a warm embrace. Miriam inhaled the familiar scent of Tilly's perfume, pressed her cheek against the well-known softness of Tilly's cheek. She swallowed a knot of sadness mixed with nostalgia. She had missed this, she thought, this enveloping affection that welcomed you back, that showed you were missed.

She hadn't felt a mother's arms around her since she had left this place, her second home.

Miriam squeezed her eyes against the sudden pain as more memories returned, and hugged Tilly as tightly as she dared.

"Oh, little girl, we sure missed you. We did." Tilly rocked her lightly, then pulled away, unabashedly wiping her eyes. "Look at you now. What a beautiful girl you've turned out to be. You're so tall. So old."

Miriam blinked her own tears away, far too conscious of Jake watching them. It shouldn't have mattered, but she felt his disapproval as strongly as she felt Tilly's love.

She knew she had been in the wrong, keeping herself from this dear person. This dear second mother who had dried her tears and hugged her even more than her own mother had.

Miriam felt ashamed. She had known this was going to be a difficult trip. She just hadn't counted on the guilt that would come with it.

Chapter 2

"*Y*ou smell like dirt, Daddy."

Jake smiled down at his daughter as he washed his hands, then bent over at the waist to wash his face and neck. "I was working on the tractor in the fields."

"Your hair is dirty, too."

Jake glanced at his reflection in the mirror, shoving his hands through his thick wavy hair. It needed to be cut. He paused, looking at himself critically, trying to see himself through Miriam's eyes. Then he wondered why he should care.

Miriam Spencer.

He drew a deep, tired breath, wishing away the jolt he had felt when he had first realized the identity of the very elegant woman standing on the side of the road. Now she sat in his kitchen, chatting with Tilly and Fred, who, even though she hadn't even bothered sending them so much as a postcard, were delighted to see her.

He felt like the older son in the parable of the prodigal son. He should be glad she was back, but he just wished he knew why she had come. He doubted it was to settle on the farm to raise wheat and canola. Miriam wasn't a country girl any longer. And it wasn't hard to see. Though her clothes were casual, they had an elegance that quietly stated their cost.

High.

He remembered the first time he had seen the new Miriam. Paula had shown him a fashion magazine, and Miriam was on the front cover—her tip-tilted eyes gleaming with gold eyeshadow, her full mouth glistening with coral lipstick. Her once unruly hair shining, curled and artfully tousled. Neither that person, nor the casually elegant girl now sitting in his kitchen, were the Miriam he knew.

The Miriam who would sometimes wear a T-shirt backward, who wouldn't care if her jeans were ripped or patched.

The Miriam he had once loved.

"What's the matter, Daddy? You look sad."

Jake pulled himself back to the present, and, squatting down, put himself level with his daughter. "I'm just tired, Pip. And hungry for some of Grandma's supper."

"That sure is a pretty lady that is here," she said solemnly, her hands on her father's shoulders.

Jake remembered the comment Taryn had made while they were standing on the porch. "What did you mean when you said you saw that lady's picture in Mommy's book? What book?"

"Mommy's book. You know." Taryn shook her head at her father's obtuseness. "Me and Grandma found it in the attic."

"I'd like to see that book when I tuck you in." He was curious but knew it would have to wait.

Jake gave her a quick hug, and, holding her tiny hand, walked back down the hallway.

"Your supper is on the table, son." Tilly smiled at Jake as he sat. "Taryn, you should run and get your pajamas on. It's getting late."

Taryn dropped her head, her fingers fiddling restlessly with each other, her lip beginning to curl in a classic pout.

"But I wanna talk to the lady," she mumbled, lifting her eyes briefly to her father.

Jake frowned at his daughter. She got the unspoken command and, sighing, turned and left.

Miriam was already ensconced on the bench against the wall, a cup of tea in front of her. Fred sat beside her, bringing Miriam up to date on what had happened in Waylen while she'd been gone.

"Here you go, son." Tilly set a plate of warmed-up food in front of him—fried chicken, creamed peas, mashed potatoes, and applesauce on the side. His mouth watered at the sight. "And here are your messages." Tilly set an assortment of papers in front of him with scribbled names and numbers. "I should charge you secretarial fees," Tilly joked. "Melissa Toews phoned three times. Said it was important. Was grumbling that she couldn't get you on your cell phone."

Jake stifled a groan. Melissa could never be accused of being coy, he thought, flipping through the messages.

"Do you want the phone?" Fred asked, reaching behind him to take the phone off the cradle.

"I don't feel like phoning anyone tonight." Jake set the papers aside. He often took care of his business during supper, but tonight he didn't feel like it. All of them could wait. Especially Melissa.

"Are you sure you don't want any supper, Miriam?" Tilly asked her, setting a cup of coffee in front of Jake.

"I'm fine, thanks." Miriam smiled gently at Tilly and rested her elbows on the table, avoiding Jake's look. "This kitchen looks the same as I remember it."

He wondered why she had come back. Then, pushing aside his own thoughts, he bowed his head in prayer. He pulled in a slow breath, willing the negative thoughts away. He slowly let himself be open to God, thanking him for the food, for the day. He paused a moment, his thoughts turning to the girl sitting at the same table, and he sent up a prayer for Miriam, as well.

He opened his eyes and subconsciously sought her out. She was watching him, her soft brown eyes full of a sorrow he hadn't seen there before. But with a blink of her long, thick eyelashes, it was gone.

"And how is your mother?" Tilly asked, leaning forward. "We haven't heard from her, either, since both of you left."

Jake stopped chewing, his own curiosity piqued by Tilly's straightforward but softly spoken question.

Miriam looked down, running her finger along the handle of the earthenware mug in front of her. "She died six months ago in Toronto. She'd had a stroke and was just getting worse. I think death was a relief for her."

Jake felt sudden empathy. He had never cared for Miriam's mother, but he knew that Miriam had loved her. He wanted to catch Miriam's gaze, to tell her he understood, but after his barely restrained hostility toward her in his truck, he felt he had no right.

"Oh, dear." Tilly reached across the table and caught Miriam's hand in her own. "I'm sorry to hear that. We never heard a thing…" Tilly let the sentence trail off. She paused, then asked, "How are you doing with it?"

Miriam reached up and carefully wiped her eyes. "It's still hard, but I think she was glad to go."

Jake heard the sorrow in her voice and wondered who had comforted her when it happened. Was there someone important to her who had been with her? She was only twenty-seven years old. Old enough to be independent, yet quite young to be without either parent.

And why hadn't she told them?

"So, now you're here for a visit?"

Miriam nodded again. "I'm only here for a while, but it's nice to be back."

"And now your car is broken down." Tilly shook her head,

clucking sympathetically. "Well, don't you worry. Fred and Jake will make sure it gets to the garage."

"It's not necessary. I can call a tow truck," Miriam protested.

Fred looked up from his paper, frowning. "That's not neighborly. That will cost you money."

Miriam said nothing to that.

"It's okay where it is right now," Jake said, pushing his potatoes around on his plate. "Tomorrow we can tow it into town and take it to Denny's Auto Parts. All it needs is a new radiator, I'm assuming."

"It was leaking already in Winnipeg," Miriam said quietly. "I think all they did was put some stop-leak stuff in it."

"Do you want me to take care of it, Jake?" Fred offered.

Jake shook his head. "You're finally out of bed. I don't think you should overdo it."

"But you'll fall behind in the field work," Fred protested. "You won't have time to run around."

"Look, I can call a tow truck," Miriam interrupted. "I don't want to put anyone out."

"Actually, you can't," Fred put in. "I heard that Lonnie's truck broke down as well. He can't give you a tow for a few days."

Miriam bit her lip, as if thinking.

"It's not a problem." Jake tried to sound nonchalant. Actually, it *was* a problem. He was getting ready to seed, and taking Miriam's car to the garage would use up a good half day. He didn't really have the time but knew it would look churlish not to help.

It would work out.

Miriam tried once more to protest, but Jake simply shook his head, cutting off further discussion.

"Do you want any dessert?" Tilly asked when Jake was done.

"No thanks, Mom. I'm full." He smiled up at her. "It was delicious, though."

Tilly stroked his hair the way she always did, and for a moment, Jake was conscious of Miriam's deep brown eyes watching them. He felt a little foolish. Not too many men his age had mothers who still stroked their hair. But he had never protested, not even as a young man.

Whenever his brother Simon would come for a visit from the stricter home he'd been placed in, Tilly treated him the same way she treated Jake. Like they were both Fred and Tilly's own sons. Neither he nor Simon had received much of a mother's love growing up. Their natural mother had given them up when they were both four after their biological father had died. The adoption was a closed one, so they knew nothing about her. After their adoptive father died, and they were placed in a new home, Simon wanted to go looking for her. When he ran away from their home numerous times to do just that, they both got moved. Simon ran away again, but when Jake was brought to Fred and Tilly's place, he was done running after a dream. He and Simon had a bitter fight about finding their mother.

Simon said that Jake would never hear from him again.

And Jake hadn't.

Each time he saw Taryn, he wondered anew how his mother could give up her own children and not even leave them with a name to track down. It was as if she wanted them swept out of her life.

But the hurt over the silence between them lingered. However, when he finally tried to connect with his brother, it was to discover that Simon no longer had that number. But, in all fairness, Jake's had changed as well. Technology and cell phones had created a communications abyss.

Then, five months ago, Jake got a phone call from a nurse named Caitlin Severn who had Simon as a patient.

She encouraged Jake to go see Simon. To tell him how much his brother had changed and yearned to reconnect.

Jake had overcome his own wounded pride and traveled to Vancouver to see him. The reunion was stilted at first, but blood and the desire to be together won out. They both vowed to never let this happen again.

They shared what little information they'd discovered about their mother. A place she had stayed at, then moved away from. A ghost slipping through life.

And now she was gone.

"Hi, Daddy. Here I am." Taryn stood in front of him, her face shiny from washing, her hair still damp.

Precious present breaking into the painful past.

She twirled around in her new, frilly nightgown, the ruffle on the bottom dragging on the floor.

"You look beautiful." Jake pulled her on his lap, tucking her under his chin.

"Not as beautiful as her." Taryn pointed to Miriam with a giggle. Jake couldn't help but look at Miriam, who was now gazing wistfully at Taryn. He didn't acknowledge Taryn's comment—at least not out loud. And as he watched the play of emotions on Miriam's face, he wondered if she had any regrets about her decisions. If the fame and fortune she had acquired satisfied her.

He turned back to his daughter, his heart full of gratitude, thankful that despite how things had turned out, he had his beloved Taryn.

"So, Pip, it's bedtime," he said quietly. "Kiss Grandpa and Grandma good-night, and I'll tuck you in."

"Okay." She lifted her shoulders, releasing an exaggerated sigh. She slipped off his lap and walked around the table to kiss Tilly and then Fred.

For a moment, Jake was afraid she was going to give Miriam a kiss as well, but shyness won out. Instead, Taryn just waggled her fingers at Miriam.

"Good night, Taryn. Sweet dreams," Miriam said softly, waving back.

"Okay. I will." Taryn smiled, then ran off through the hallway toward the stairs, Jake right behind.

When Paula and Jake had first married, they had lived in a mobile home on the property. However, after Paula had died, Jake had brought Taryn here so often that she'd ended up getting her own room. Eventually, Jake had started eating supper here, and soon, the mobile home had been sold.

Now they all lived here in a house that was getting too big for Tilly to clean. But she refused to move to a smaller house in town, and Jake had to admit that it worked better for him, as well.

At the bottom of the stairs, Taryn stopped, holding up her arms for the first step in their bedtime routine.

He loved this house, he mused as he walked slowly up the broad stairs holding his little girl. As a foster child, he'd been blessed to end up here, and he knew it.

Though his mother had given Simon and Jake up, he was always thankful that they had been adopted by a single man, Tom Steele. He had given them a safe and secure home for seven years. His death had been a severe blow, and Jake knew that the loss of Tom tended to make him overprotective of Fred. He didn't want to lose another father.

"Stop, Daddy. I want to see the pictures."

Jake smiled and did as his daughter commanded. The Prins' had a veritable gallery on the wall, and Taryn always had to stop to check them out. Jake didn't mind. He was so thankful for the legacy his daughter received through Fred and Tilly that it was doubly important to him that she knew where she came from. His vague memories of his mother didn't include a father, let alone grandparents. At times he still resented that but realized that, in Tom Steele, and later in Fred and Tilly, God had made up for the lack.

"There's my mommy." Taryn leaned forward, pointing out

their wedding picture. Taryn always lingered the longest here, even though she barely remembered Paula. Taryn had been only two when Paula died, and unaware of the circumstances surrounding her mother's death. Paula had been an inattentive mother at best and hadn't spent a lot of time at home. Jake often regretted his marriage, but he had never, ever regretted Taryn.

"And this is Uncle Simon and Aunty Caitlin." Taryn pointed with a pudgy finger to a smiling couple, their arms around each other. The wedding picture had been taken outside against a backdrop of cherry trees in full bloom. The filtered sun highlighted their features and enhanced the love that radiated from them.

"When I get bigger"—Taryn stopped as her mouth stretched open in a big yawn—"I want to be a nurse, just like Aunty Caitlin, and help her in her hospital in Na...Nomimo," she continued, snuggling into her father's neck.

"Nanaimo," Jake corrected, giving his daughter a tight hug. "That's a good thing to be, sweetie. But if you don't get your sleep, you won't grow, and then you can't be a nurse."

A night-light shed a soft glow over Taryn's room. Jake lay Taryn down on her bed, careful not to disturb the row of stuffed animals that sat along the side, next to the wall. He tucked her in and sat beside her, his arms on either side of her shoulders.

Taryn smiled up at her father, and a wave of pure, sweet love washed over Jake. He bent over and gave her another quick kiss. "Time for your prayers."

"We have to pray for Grandpa, don't we?" Taryn asked, her soft hazel eyes shining up at him in the muted light.

"Yes, we want him to stay healthy, don't we?"

"Should we pray for Miriam?"

Jake felt his heart skip at her name. He took a quick breath, frowning down at his daughter. "What did you say?"

"I *asked*," Taryn began, putting emphasis on the last word

as if to show Jake that he was being particularly obtuse, "if I should pray for Miriam."

"You barely know her. Which reminds me, tell me about this book you found?"

Taryn sat up like a shot and, shifting around, pulled a worn scrapbook from under her pillow. She handed it to him.

"It has pictures of you in it." Taryn smiled, eager for the reprieve from sleep. "And pictures of my mommy and pictures of the pretty lady. Miriam. I'll show you." Taryn reached for the book, and, reluctantly, Jake gave it back. He didn't like the idea of Taryn living in the past, creating fantasies about Paula. But he also knew that it wasn't fair to take what little she had away.

Taryn flipped quickly through the pages of pictures from high school—a few of them of Jake—then she stopped and tilted the book in his direction. Jake felt his heart stop as he looked directly at a picture of Miriam.

In the picture, she wore a mauve silk dress held up with narrow, jeweled straps. Diamonds sparkled at her neck, her ears, her fingers, all discreetly proclaiming "expensive." Her mouth was quirked in what he knew was her cynical smile, her head tilted back as if she were laughing at some private joke. Her blonde hair was pulled back from her face, loose tendrils accenting her high cheekbones and the exotic tilt of her eyes. A slickly dressed man wearing a tuxedo stood beside her, his arm resting in a proprietary manner on her shoulder.

"Why did Mommy have pictures of Miriam in her book?"

Jake blinked, pulling himself back to the present. "She used to be your mommy's best friend," Jake murmured, turning the page to find yet another color picture of Miriam. It was a makeup advertisement. Miriam's face took up the whole page, her head angled slightly downward, her eyes glancing up, her shining mouth holding the hint of a smile. Jake swallowed as he stared at the picture. It was Miriam, and yet not. How many times had he seen that look on her face—

across a classroom, in the hallways of school; whenever she would tease him, flirt with him?

"I want to show Miriam the pictures, okay?" Taryn gathered up the book and made to jump out of bed, but Jake stopped her.

"No," he said firmly, taking the book away from her and setting it on the bedside table. "I'm sure Miriam has seen these pictures herself. And you need to sleep." He pulled the blankets up around her and tucked her in. She said her prayers, and Jake said them with her.

Each evening, he thanked God for the precious gift entrusted to him. And as he did most evenings, he promised he would do everything he could to make sure she would have a home as secure and loving as the one he had received through Fred and Tilly.

"…and be with Miriam, my mommy's friend." Jake felt a start at the sound of Taryn praying for Miriam as she said she would, but he kept quiet, not wanting to draw any more attention to Miriam.

He waited until Taryn was done, then bent over and kissed her gently. He paused at the door to look once more, closed it behind him, and went downstairs to face Miriam.

He heard them laughing and stopped just behind the door, listening, remembering other times.

Like the first time he had seen Miriam.

He had been sitting, hunched over, on Fred and Tilly's picnic table, staring out at the view below—a young, sullen boy of fourteen, brought to his third foster home in as many years and recently separated from his brother Simon. The social worker had been inside the house, talking to Fred and Tilly. He hadn't wanted to hear what she had to say.

So, he had stayed outside, trying to appreciate the flow of the land that stretched out below him, the open spaces compared to the cramped foster home he's just come from.

Bitterly resenting his brother's actions that had brought him here.

But more importantly, wondering how he was going to survive in a house with only two old people for company.

Then a skinny girl had ridden up on her horse and jumped off. She'd tied it to a post by the back gate and boldly walked up to him, retying the shoelace that held her ponytail in place. She'd asked who he was and what he was doing sitting at Uncle Fred and Aunt Tilly's picnic table.

When he ignored her, she just shrugged and waltzed on into the house, like she lived there.

A few minutes later, she skipped outside and without asking his permission, sat beside him on the table.

To his surprise, she said nothing to him. Just sat there.

Together, they watched the sun going down, felt the soft chill that accompanied the fall evenings drifting over the yard.

The social worker came out later, accompanied by Fred and Tilly. She stopped in her tracks when she saw Miriam and spun around, asking Fred and Tilly who she was.

"Just the neighbor girl," they said. "She comes over a lot."

The social worker nodded and then stopped by Jake. Laying her hand on his shoulder, she bent down to his height —an older woman talking to an angry young man. "This is a good place, Jake," she whispered. "Don't wreck things for yourself."

Jake had ignored her, staring past her at the setting sun. Social workers were always full of advice and, as far as he was concerned, misconceptions. The fact that he had been in so many homes had more to do with Simon's constant running away than with Jake's behavior. But he didn't want to get into that. It hurt to think of Simon. It was the first time they had been separated. So, he only nodded and said nothing, wondering where his brother had ended up and when he would see him again. He knew it was a waste of time to ask the social worker. She would give him some vague answer about waiting to see if they settled in.

Then she left.

He thought Fred and Tilly were going to come over and send Miriam away. Thought they were going to sit with him. Talk to him.

Instead, all Tilly did was gently touch his shoulder and tell him that supper was waiting for him when he was ready to come inside.

Giving him a small measure of control.

To his surprise and dismay, Miriam stayed beside him. He had wanted to be alone, but she wouldn't leave. After a while, though, it didn't matter as much. She had been pretty quiet.

Tilly came out and brought them a glass of orange juice and then returned to the house.

Miriam slurped her juice down, then turned to him and started talking. He had known her silence was too good to be true. She asked questions, the basic ones—What's your name? How old are you? Where did you live before?

His replies were terse. He had answered enough questions before this placement to add twenty more pages to his already thick file. Everyone knew everything about him, so the trick was to hold back as much as he could for as long as he could.

Miriam chatted about the school, the town, Tilly and Fred. She said nothing about her own mother. In fact, at first, he thought she didn't even have one.

When it seemed she was finished, she took their empty glasses back to the house. When she came back, all she did was wave goodbye, jump on her horse, and ride away, leaving a bemused Jake behind.

Miriam came often to Fred and Tilly's. She sought him out at school, introduced him to her many friends. At first, he resisted her advances, but she persisted, undaunted by his surly attitude.

Slowly, persistently, she wore his defenses down. And he began to enjoy being with her.

She had an easy way with people, a self-deprecating wit and a love of life that he found compelling and infectious.

He ended up falling desperately in love with her. And she with him.

Miriam had filled the empty spaces that being abandoned by their mother and his anger with Simon had carved out of him. Her unconditional love had shown him that there were things worth making sacrifices for. For the first time in years, he had opened himself up to another person, had made himself vulnerable. He had trusted her.

They spent hours just talking, being together, sharing dreams and plans. Jake often felt unworthy of her.

Miriam often spoke of her mother and how important it was that they keep their relationship a secret from her. And they did. Jake knew what he was: a foster child with an uncertain future.

It hurt to think of what they had once had. To realize that the elegant woman who was chatting in his kitchen was even further removed from him now than she was then. So much had changed in each of their lives.

He stepped into the kitchen. Fred was describing an incident he had had with a bull, many years ago.

"...And Tilly thinks I'm waving to her to come closer, and she comes roaring up with the truck and scares the bull. He takes off past me down the road and with him went all the plans for the day. We finally got him corralled at midnight."

Miriam had her hand over her mouth; her eyes sparkled, and her shoulders shook in time to her chuckles.

Jake stopped, unable to look away.

This was the Miriam he had fallen in love with. *This* was the Miriam he had promised he would stay with forever. Not that overly made-up woman with the fake smile whom he had just seen in the photo. Not the defensive woman who had sat with him in the truck all the way here.

Then she glanced sidelong, her hand slowly dropped, and her gaze skittered away.

He felt as if he had broken the moment.

"Taryn safely in bed?" Tilly asked, smiling up at him.

Jake nodded and sat at the table, suddenly feeling like the odd man out. He tried not to look at the clock but couldn't help it.

Miriam caught him looking; she carefully put her spoon back in her coffee cup and folded the napkin Tilly had given her. Preparations for leaving.

"What's the rush, girl?" Fred asked, as Miriam eased herself from behind the table.

"I should go. It's been a long day of driving." She picked up her mug, took it to the counter, and set it down with a muted *clink.*

"Are we going to see you again?" Tilly asked as she got up herself.

Miriam turned to face Tilly and nodded. "Of course. Once I get my car fixed, that is."

"Oh, nonsense. I can come over." Tilly stopped, glancing at Jake, then back to Miriam. "What about your house? Is there any food there?"

"I bought some groceries, but unfortunately, they're still in my car—"

"Don't be silly, girl, I'll give you some," Tilly interjected.

Miriam hesitated, and Jake sensed she was in a dilemma. Either she accepted charity from Tilly, or she put him out by asking him to return to her car.

"Did you have any suitcases?" he asked her, feeling foolish that he had never thought of that when he picked her up.

"It's in my car," she said, lifting her head.

"Well, it's not far down the road. I'll drive you back, and

you can get your other stuff. Besides, your groceries will spoil if we don't get them."

"Thank you," she said with a gracious tilt of her head. She turned back to Tilly. "Thanks for the tea." She stopped there, her voice trembling, as if she could say nothing more.

Tilly walked over and gave Miriam another hug. "It's such a treat to see you again," she said, pulling back, cupping Miriam's young face with her old, lined hands. "I'm so glad you decided to come back."

Fred, too, walked over and gave her a hug. But Jake could see that even that small movement tired him out.

Miriam had noticed it, too. Her eyes were full of concern. "You make sure you get enough rest," she said to Fred, holding his hand between hers.

"You sound just like Tilly." He gave her a shake of his head. "I'll be fine." He reached up and stroked her cheek, much the way Tilly had done to Jake.

In that moment, Jake realized that, despite a ten-year absence, Miriam shared something special with Fred and Tilly. And for a moment, he was envious.

Chapter 3

"So," Jake said vaguely as he spun the steering wheel, still not looking directly at her. "What really brings you back here?"

The question, spoken in a defensive tone, hung between them. For a moment, Miriam was tempted to let it slip past her. Ignore it.

But she sensed the question had been burning inside of him, and he had a right to know.

Instead, she waited a beat, as if to establish some sort of conversational control. Then, reminding herself she had nothing to explain or apologize for, simply said, "I came back to sell my farm."

Jake's head snapped around, and he stared at her, then looked quickly away. "This is a surprise."

Miriam didn't doubt it. Fred and Jake had rented the land associated with her mother's farm since her father died. But all their dealings had been at arm's length through a lawyer Edna had hired.

"I don't know if you're interested in buying it," she continued. "Because of our rental agreement, you and Fred will have right of first refusal."

Jake blew out his breath and laughed shortly. "I would be. Unfortunately, I can't afford to buy it now. Financially, I'm stretched as far as I can go."

Miriam felt a stab of dismay. She had hoped he would buy it, had hoped he could keep farming it. That somehow, something that had once belonged to her would now belong to him, creating a vague kind of connection. Though she wasn't sure why. "That's too bad," she said, threading her fingers together in her lap.

"At least we agree on that." His words were clipped, and once again, Miriam sensed his anger.

But she was too tired to say anything back.

"What happens once you sell the farm?" Jake continued.

Miriam pressed her lips together, willing away her fatigue. She had walked down catwalks in Milan, had modeled famous designers' fashions with aplomb and self-confidence. Surely, she could handle a farmer who needed a shave. "I go back east and put Waylen behind me."

He sucked in a quick breath but, thankfully, said nothing more.

Gravel rattled against the undercarriage as they drove down the road, the oppressive silence of two people unwilling to talk to each other filling the cab.

She was thankful it was a short trip to her car. As Jake pulled up beside it, Miriam dug the keys out of her purse. She climbed out of the truck and unlocked the car's trunk.

Jake was beside her and reached in and wordlessly pulled out her suitcase. Miriam took out a small cosmetics bag and closed the trunk.

"This is it?"

Miriam nodded and walked around the car to get her groceries.

"You travel pretty light."

"I've made enough airline connections with my clothes headed off to Istanbul while I was going to New York. I've learned to take everything I need with me." Miriam juggled the grocery bags in one hand while she locked the door with the other.

"I don't think this car is going anywhere," Jake said.

Miriam frowned up at him. "What do you mean?"

"This is a dead-end road. You hardly need to lock the car."

Miriam tried not to smile but couldn't help it. It did look silly to lock up a crippled car on a deserted road. "City habits, I guess," she said, chancing a glance up at him.

Mistake. He was smiling now, his features relaxed. He looked devastating.

She forced herself to look away. "Well, that should do it." Miriam straightened her shoulders and dropped her groceries in the box of Jake's pickup, frustrated at how quickly the old feelings she had had for him returned. It was as if she had never been gone. As if she had never spent time with any man other than this tall farmer of few words.

"You might want to put your suitcase in the front. I hauled feed with this truck the other day."

"A little extra oats and soy never hurt a girl," she said quickly.

Jake dropped the suitcase in the box beside her groceries. When he glanced up at her, she caught a curious expression slipping over his handsome, rugged features. Regret? Longing? Enough to make Miriam's heart skip.

Silly girl, she castigated herself. *You're wasting your time on this one. He is out of reach for you.* She got in the truck, slammed the door, and buckled up. The trip back to her house was as quiet as the trip to her car had been.

Dusk was gathering by the time they drove down the driveway. Miriam had so hoped to see her old house in the light. But as they pulled into the yard, she caught darkened glimpses of overgrown grass, tangled shrubs, and flower gardens full of weeds, and she wondered if she really wanted to know.

"My mother and I paid someone to keep this place up. What happened?"

"Velma Rogers? She only took care of the inside of the house. Said she wasn't paid for more. We tried to keep the outside fixed up, but we didn't have time," Jake said, his voice brusque. "We did check on the house every few months, just to make sure everything was still working. Your mother must have had the lawyer who collected the rent take care of the power and gas bills."

Miriam nodded, then slowly got out of the truck and looked around. It was unkempt enough in the half-light; she didn't know if she wanted to see it in the unforgiving sunshine.

"Thanks for driving me here." Waves of exhaustion made her legs wobble. She clung to the open truck door. "Don't worry about the car. I can call another towing company."

"That's okay," he said, turning and getting out of the truck. He handed her the grocery bags, then pulled her suitcase out of the back. "I'll come by tomorrow, and you can help me take it into town."

"No, really, I know how busy this time of the year is. The last thing you need to do is cart me around. Please." She felt a moment's warmth kindle in her heart at his thoughtfulness.

"You heard what my dad said. Lance can't come for a couple of days, and he's the nearest driver. I'm sure you'll want your car working as soon as possible. I'll tow it."

Before she could formulate another feeble protest, he strode ahead of her to the back door and stood aside so she could open it.

The sound of the door opening echoed hollowly through the house, and Miriam felt a wave of nostalgia. It was so familiar, so much a part of her youth. How many times had she opened this very door and gone running in to throw her backpack down on the porch floor, asking if there was anything to eat?

With her free hand, Miriam flicked the switch by the back door, and light flooded the porch. There was a faint musty smell.

Miriam walked up the three steps into the kitchen, stifling a cry of dismay as she looked past it to the living room. All the furniture was draped with white sheets; pictures had been taken off the wall and stacked in corners of the room. It all looked desolate and distinctly un-homey. She set the groceries on the counter, hoping the refrigerator worked.

Jake walked over to the taps and turned them. "Water's still okay, although you might want to drain the hot water out of the tank. I'm sure it's pretty stale. We did it at Eastertime, but that's the last time I went through this place. Velma had asked me to go over everything this fall again."

"Thanks, Jake. I'll do that." Her head was starting to buzz, and she wanted nothing more than to have a nice warm shower and crawl into bed. One look around the house, though, told her she had other things to do first.

"Do you want some help…" Jake let the sentence trail off.

"No, thanks. I'll be fine." She yearned for some time to herself, some time to gather her scattered thoughts. She wanted him gone. She wanted this cold formality between them to end, and it would only happen when he left.

Jake nodded, one hand caught in the back pocket of his blue jeans. "I'll walk through the house once, to make sure everything's okay. Where do you want your suitcase?"

"Just leave it here, please."

The sound of his boots thumping through the house was muffled by the cloths draping all the furniture. Shivering, Miriam walked through the kitchen into the darkened living room, hugging herself against the chill of the house. The room here had a feeling of abandonment. Loneliness.

With a muted rumble, the furnace started up.

Jake returned and paused in the arched doorway between the kitchen and the living room, looking around. "Well, I'll be going. Are you sure you're going to be all right?"

Miriam turned to him, nodding. "Thanks for everything. I'm sorry to be such a pain…" She let the sentence drift off as their eyes met.

The backlight from the kitchen silhouetted him, and she couldn't help but acknowledge his appeal. He was taller, broader. Not the young man she had left behind, but a man who had had his own experiences. He had buried a wife and now had a child, ran a farm, and took care of parents who looked so much older to Miriam than they had when she left. He was a stranger to her. A stranger with his own heartaches and his own responsibilities.

"I'll be by sometime tomorrow to take your car into town." Jake scratched his head, as if he wanted to say more. Then, with a shrug, he turned and left before she could protest again.

Miriam walked to the window of the darkened room and watched through the large picture window as Jake started his truck, the headlights stabbing the darkness.

She lay her head against the cold glass, letting the emotions of the day flow over her. Then, against her will, she felt tears gather. She didn't know precisely what she cried for; she only knew that she had felt a deep sadness closing in on her since she'd first seen Jake, then Fred and Tilly. All the memories of her mother's death returned, hard and fast. Telling Jake, Fred, and Tilly had been like reliving that stark moment when she'd felt her mother's hand go limp in her own.

Once again, she replayed those moments after the funeral, when all the temporary supports—the nursing home staff, the undertaker, the minister who performed the service—had slowly fallen away, and she'd realized she was all alone.

She had no one who cared. No one who mattered. The

men she had met treated her like a trophy to be won and shown. Other men treated her like a commodity—a model, a face to sell their product.

There had been only one man in her life. Ever.

She felt another wave of sorrow thinking about Jake and his daughter. A daughter borne by her best friend.

She cried for the loss of the dreams that both she and Jake had spun during those innocent long-ago evenings, and for the lives that reality had changed.

The window was cool and soothing against her hot forehead, and slowly, the tears subsided. They always did. And as always, reality returned.

She straightened, pulled her shoulders back, lifted her chin.

Automatic movements that reasserted, at least outwardly, her confidence.

She had much to do if she wanted to sleep here tonight.

THE NEXT MORNING, Jake turned into Miriam's driveway, the entrance of which was barely visible in the driving rain, unable to stop a gentle lift of his heart at the thought of seeing her again.

Yesterday, the surprise of her sudden reappearance after ten years had put him on the defensive.

And no wonder. She had kept herself away from people who cared about her, himself included, he reminded himself as his truck bounced through a puddle. She had told no one what was going on in her life.

Even as Jake mentally considered a litany of her shortcomings, he knew the silence between them wasn't all on her.

And what else could he have done?

He pushed the questions aside, wondering how she had

fared last night, her first night all alone in her childhood house.

He had thought about her in this empty house during the drive back home, then again as he lay in bed, staring up at the ceiling in his room. Surprising, how easily the memories had returned. The fun times they had had. The excitement of the first moment of discovering their feelings for each other. Those first hesitant movements toward a deeper connection.

A touch. A glance.

Then, that first kiss.

Yet Miriam had been more than a girlfriend. She had been his closest friend. There had been nothing going on in his life, past or present, that she hadn't known about.

Jake sighed lightly as he came to a halt in front of Miriam's house. Too much had happened between them, and the only way to get past it was to talk about it.

But why bother, when she was selling the farm and leaving again?

Jake jumped out of the truck and ran up the walk to the house, rain slicing down on his head. He huddled deeper into his jean jacket and rapped on the door. The rain was really coming down now, a typical prairie rainstorm swishing and beating against the peeling woodwork of the house.

He rapped on the door again and then pushed it open, stepping quickly inside. As he closed the door behind him, he looked up to see Miriam come through the kitchen. She was wiping her hands on a cloth, wearing an apron over a pair of loose cargo pants that hung low on her hips and a T-shirt that barely ended above the waistband.

"Hi, there," she said, her expression neutral. "I wasn't sure when you were coming. Did you want to leave right away?"

"If you don't mind." Jake slicked his damp hair back from his face, wiping the moisture from his cheeks with the shoulder of his jacket, unable to take his eyes off her. Her hair looked tousled, her feet were bare, and unlike yesterday, today she wore no makeup.

The effect was captivating. She looked younger, fresher, and more approachable. More like the Miriam he had once known.

His heart stirred in response, his pulse quickened. Then she lifted her soft brown eyes to his, and in that moment, they seemed connected, pulled together by an invisible cord, by memories and old feelings that had never been resolved.

He blinked and forced his gaze away, breaking the tie. "I'll be waiting in the truck for you," he said, looking past her at the wall behind her. "You might want to wear some boots if you have them."

He saw Miriam nod and take a step back. "I'll be right out," she said quietly. When she turned and walked away, he watched her go, noting the graceful sway of her hips.

Pull yourself together, Jake, he berated himself. *She's not for you, and she's not sticking around.* With a shake of his head, he left the house.

He needed to get out more.

Trouble was, he had no desire to date again.

He had a foster father who wasn't feeling well, an older foster mother who couldn't do as much as she used to, a small daughter he never felt he spent enough time with, and a large farm to run on his own. His love life had been luckless, to put it mildly. Women were a complication he could do without. He had Taryn. She was his first responsibility. Tilly and Fred were his second, and together that was more than enough for him.

He was glad he had decided at the last minute to leave Taryn behind. The almost reverential tone she used when talking about Miriam made him uneasy. Besides, Taryn had lately taken to talking about getting a mommy, like this was an item Jake could take care of for her in a minute.

He knew Taryn, and he was afraid that her fascination

would translate into simple math. Miriam was single, Jake was single. One plus one equals a mommy for Taryn. And despite the fancies of his own foolish heart, he couldn't imagine a more unsuitable candidate for the job than Miriam.

Jake watched as Miriam picked her way through the puddles on the driveway to the passenger side of the truck. To his surprise, she wore a bright red rain coat and hiking boots. He reached across the seat and opened the door. Miriam stepped in, a cloud of sweet-smelling perfume filling the cab as she shot Jake a grateful smile.

Jake twisted the key in the ignition and tried to ignore that irresistible smell that telegraphed her presence.

The only sounds in the cab were the hum of the heater fan and the slap of windshield wipers on the window. Just like yesterday, silence lay between them.

And suddenly, Jake was tired of it. "How long do you plan on staying here?"

"I figure about two weeks. I was hoping to go to a real estate agent today."

"Do you think that's long enough to sell your farm?" Jake tried to inject a casual note into his voice. It made him angry that she could so easily talk of selling her farm. The idea bothered him for so many reasons.

"Probably not, but it will get things started. It just needs to be listed, and whoever I go with can take it from there. The rest I can probably do via e-mail. Besides, I could only spare that much time here. I have work to go back to."

"Modeling?"

"Yes."

Her quiet reply made Jake take a chance and look at her again. She was looking straight ahead, her mouth pressed into a firm line, her fingers wrapped tightly around each other.

"If you don't mind my intruding, you don't seem too eager about that."

Miriam laughed shortly, pressing her thumbs together. "It pays the bills."

Jake looked back at the road again. He was sure it did. Paula had often spoken with outright envy of how much she figured Miriam made, doing what she did.

He sighed, tapping his thumbs lightly on the steering wheel as he tried to find something to say. He felt awkward and gauche, and he didn't like it.

But she wasn't the Miriam he used to tease; she wasn't the Miriam whose laugh would bubble up at the lamest joke. Despite his original antipathy toward her, he felt old feelings resurfacing, and through new-old eyes, he saw a sadness in her.

They turned a corner, and there was her car.

Jake stopped and frowned over a new problem. Town was west and Miriam's car was facing east. And the road was too narrow to pull it around and not get the tow rope tangled.

"We'll have to tow it back to the house to get it turned around," he said, thinking out loud.

"Why don't you pull it to the next approach and turn in?" Miriam suggested.

Jake rubbed his thumb along his chin, shaking his head. "Then I won't be able to back out."

"How about pushing it around? It's just a small car."

Jake chewed on his thumbnail, considering.

"You still chew your nails?" Miriam asked, her voice tinged with laughter.

Jake jerked his head around, suddenly self-conscious. "I don't chew my nails," he said, dropping his hand.

"That's what you always said." Miriam smiled again at the shared memory, and once again, their eyes met.

Why couldn't he look away? Why couldn't he just casually return the smile and turn his head? It was just mechanics—lift mouth in casual way, move neck muscles. Mission accomplished.

But other messages were ruling his head right now. Like how much narrower her face was than before, how the light caught her high cheekbones, accenting them. He suddenly noticed a delicate fan of wrinkles from her eyes, smudges of shadows beneath them. There was a weariness to her features that he hadn't noticed yesterday.

Jake took a deep breath, pulling himself back to the dilemma at hand.

"It's not a big car," she said again. "We could push it around."

Jake considered this new suggestion and then, with a shrug, said, "We can try."

Jake jumped out of the truck, shut the door, and walked over to the car. Miriam was beside him.

"I could push, and you could work the steering," Jake said quickly. "The road isn't too muddy yet, so we should be okay."

"Let's try it." She pulled the keys out of her pocket and unlocked the car, then put the key in the ignition and put the car into neutral. She positioned herself, gave Jake a nod, and on his count, they started pushing. The car was small, just as Miriam had said, but it was also low. Jake had to bend far down to get any kind of leverage.

"Do they get any lower?" he grunted as he strained to move it.

"Not much," Miriam said.

"I'm surprised you didn't bottom out on these roads."

"You always"—Miriam took a breath and pushed harder —"talk this much…when…you're working?"

Keeps me from thinking, he thought.

The car was moving slowly, but fortunately, it was turning in the right direction. The road might just be wide enough.

Jake was bent over so far that he couldn't see what was happening, so when Miriam called out, "Stop, stop," he didn't know why. He looked up just in time to see her jump into the car. He was totally unprepared for the jolt as the car came to an abrupt halt. His hands slipped down the trunk of the wet car, his feet slipped on the wet gravel. The next thing he knew, he was lying flat out in a dirty puddle of water, rain dripping down his neck.

He sucked his breath in and lay there a moment, to assimilate what had happened, embarrassment and the icy water seeping through his clothes, gravel digging into his face, each vying for his attention. The water won out as he shoved himself off the ground, getting his hands dirty in the process. Amazing how quickly one could go from feeling competent and in charge to humiliated and out of control.

"Are you okay?" Miriam poked her head out of the car which was now stopped. She got out, and as she took a good look at him, her hand flew up to her mouth. Her lips were pulled in and she glanced quickly down, then up again.

"You're laughing at me," he said, pulling his wet and dirty coat away from his chest, water dripping down his face. "I'm in absolute misery here, and you're standing there laughing at me."

"Sorry," she said, her voice muffled by her hand.

He saw her shoulders shake, and then, as he looked down at his soaking wet pants and coat, he started smiling himself.

Jake wiped the dirty water off his face with the cuff of his coat. He looked over at Miriam now and saw her eyes dancing. "You better stop laughing, Miriam Spencer, or your hair won't look so clean anymore."

"I'm not laughing," she said, dropping her hand, apparently forcing herself to look more serious.

But then he felt a clump of mud dislodge itself from his hair and slide down his face. Jake swiped at it, but it was too late. Now Miriam was laughing out loud, her arms clutching her midsection.

"I'm sorry," she gasped, lifting one hand as if in surrender. "I'm sorry."

Jake laughed as well. Then, shaking his head, he walked

over to the truck. "Well, you just stand there and giggle like a girl—I'm getting the rope."

He pulled the tow rope out of the back of the truck and walked over to Miriam's car. His pants were wet anyhow, so he knelt in the gravel, staring under the car with dismay.

"Can I do anything?" she asked, squatting down beside him.

"Yeah." He glanced over his shoulder, forcing himself to look serious. "You can get that little body of yours under this car and hook this on."

Miriam looked taken aback. "Okay," she said quietly, wiping her hands on her coat as if in preparation.

"Kidding." He grinned at her.

"You rat." She gave his shoulder a push, almost knocking him over.

"Don't start anything you can't finish, Mims," he said with a mock warning tone and a wink. The nickname came easily to him, and so did the wink.

Miriam's expression grew serious. "I haven't heard that in years." Miriam dropped her hand and straightened. Then she turned away. "Let me know if you need anything," she said quietly.

Jake looked down at the rope, shaking his head. *Keep your mind on the job at hand*, he reminded himself. He was surprised at how readily her old nick-name had rolled off his tongue, surprised at her response to it. With difficulty, he shrugged the memories away and bent over to find a suitable place to hook up the rope.

"You'll need to ride in the car," he said to Miriam as he got up, pleased at how casual he managed to sound. "I'll go slow, and you'll have to brake before I do. I'll touch the brakes lightly when I need you to brake, okay? I'll give you lots of time."

"Where are we going?"

"Denny's Auto Parts. I'm sure they'll have something for

you, or they'll find it. There's no dealer in town for this make of car."

She gave him a curt nod and got into the car. Jake hesitated a moment, then turned and walked back to the truck.

As he drove, Jake kept alternating between looking at the road ahead and at the car behind him, his mind on neither. He kept wondering why he had called Miriam "Mims." The name had come from a deep place he had forgotten about. He had used Mims only in times of affection.

He sighed and flicked on the radio, hoping the music would keep his mind occupied. But he couldn't forget the brief connection they'd shared when it seemed that all the ten years between them had never been.

Chapter 4

*B*y the time they got to Denny's, the rain had quit and the clouds above were breaking. The weather forecaster promised blue skies and wind tomorrow. Jake hoped that would keep up, so he could be in the fields again by Monday.

When they pulled into Denny's, a couple miles out of town, he got out of the truck, undid the wet and dirty rope, and coiled it up, while Miriam went inside. He threw the rope in the back of the truck.

"You're lucky," he heard Denny say as he walked into the office. "We just parted out a car with a rad that will fit yours."

The young man at the counter sported a tattoo on each hand, a bizarre haircut, and a full beard. Denny was a terrific mechanic, although a trifle tough—the opposite of his fellow worker, Ryan, who had short hair and was clean-shaven. They both wore grease-stained overalls and, right now, foolish grins. They were unable to keep their eyes off Miriam.

It irritated Jake for a moment. He didn't like the way they were looking at her, as if she were some exotic specimen they had never seen before.

"You done in here, Miriam?"

She glanced over her shoulder. "They said they'll have it done in a couple of hours."

"Funny. I never manage to get such quick service," Jake said, his voice laced with irony.

Denny shrugged, grinning. "You know us, Jake. We aim to please beautiful women." He leaned on the counter and glanced at Jake, his eyebrows raised at the sight of Jake's shirt and pants. "What were you doing?"

"I fell in the mud pushing Miriam's car," Jake answered tersely.

"Well, I sure appreciate the service." Miriam bestowed a polite smile on them. "Is there a place I can wait while you work on it?"

"You can sit here, or you can tell us where you will be, and we can deliver it." Ryan smiled, leaning closer.

Jake resisted the urge to roll his eyes. These two were so obvious, it was sickening.

"I think I'll go to town. I have my cell phone. You can let me know when it's done." She smiled at them both and left, leaving two dazed men staring after her.

"She looks so familiar," Denny said to Jake as the door creaked closed behind her.

"She should. We used to go to school with her. Miriam Spencer."

"That Miriam Spencer is 'Sticks' Spencer?" Denny's mouth almost dropped open. Jake felt an unaccountable surge of anger at the memory of that hated nickname. Miriam had always laughed it off, but he also knew how it bothered her.

"Wow, she sure became babe material," Denny continued, stroking his beard.

"She is quite attractive," Jake said, cringing at his own prim note.

Ryan threw him a knowing smirk. "Oh, very quite," he said with a laugh.

Jake caught the door handle, feigning nonchalance. "Well, gotta run. Let me know if anything changes with Miriam's car," he said.

"She gave us her cell number." Denny craned his neck as if to get another look at Miriam, who now stood by Jake's truck. "But I'll call you, too, just in case." Denny gave Jake a wink, as if congratulating him. "She back now?"

Jake's only reply was a shrug, uncomfortable with Denny's obvious assumption—that he and Miriam were going to try again. He knew he should correct the misconception, but he figured people would know for themselves, once Miriam was gone.

When Jake got outside, Miriam wasn't by the truck anymore. He frowned, and then he saw her walking down the road toward town.

"Miriam!" he called out. "Where are you going?"

She stopped, glancing over her shoulder. "To town."

"I'll take you," he said, stifling his exasperation. Did she really think he would just drive back to the farm, leaving her to fend for herself?

"That's okay. You don't have to."

"Come back and get in the truck," he said brusquely.

Miriam hesitated. Then, with a shrug, she turned and came back. He waited for her by the passenger side of the truck and held the door open for her.

Miriam threw him an oblique glance and got in.

Jake walked around the front and climbed awkwardly into his truck, the wet denim of his pants clinging to his legs and constricting his movements.

"Where do you want to go?" he asked as he drove out of Denny's yard.

"Doesn't matter. Is Raylene's place still around?"

"No. She moved to Denver."

"Denver? Why there?"

"I heard some cowboy in town for a rodeo caught her fancy, and she sold the place and left."

Miriam laughed at that.

"What's so funny? Can't you see old Raylene Dansers losing her heart to some old bull rider?" Jake said with mock dismay.

"Bull riders don't get that old," Miriam said, grinning.

"Actually, he was the header half of a calf-roping team. You can do that sitting down."

Miriam laughed again, and Jake felt a lightness pervade the once-heavy atmosphere. "I'll take you to the new place in town," he said impulsively. "You can see how much Waylen has changed."

Miriam looked sideways at him and, to his surprise, smiled. "Thanks, Jake. That sounds good."

A few minutes later, Jake pulled up in front of a small café that had just started up.

"Where did the bakery go?" Miriam asked, getting out of the truck.

"Moved into a new complex downtown." Jake got out and stared down at his dirty pants. He really looked like a hick compared to Miriam.

He glanced up to see Miriam smiling at him. "Don't worry about your pants. I don't care if you don't."

He made it to the door ahead of her and opened it for her.

"Still a gentleman," she said lightly as she stepped through the door.

"Tilly raised me right," he returned, following her in.

"Hey, Jake." Peter Thornton, a farmer who lived down the road, waved to Jake from his seat as they came in. "The rain send you to town this morning, too?"

"Yeah," Jake said briefly. He didn't want to stop, but small-town protocol deemed that he do so. "You done seeding yet?"

"Got another sixty acres to do." Peter leaned back in his chair and looked past him, then back to Jake with a grin. "How about you?"

"About halfway." He glanced back at Miriam, who stood just behind him, her hands clasped in front of her. He didn't want to keep her waiting through the usual give and take of farming talk. Probably would bore a cosmopolitan woman like her to tears.

"Well, take care. Talk to you later." After a casual nod, he walked across the nearly empty café to the window.

He was thankful the café was quiet this morning.

Miriam sat down at the table and looked around with a smile. "Nice place."

"They opened about a year ago. They're doing quite well," Jake said, leaning on the table.

The server was already at their table, a pot of coffee in her hand. "Menus?" she asked.

Jake shook his head. "Just a cup of coffee for me," he said.

Miriam looked up. "Thanks, I'll have the same."

They watched as the server filled their cups, then was gone again.

"You didn't used to drink coffee," Jake said, pulling his cup closer.

"I started while I was modeling. All that waiting around. Late nights and early mornings." She took a careful sip from her cup, avoiding his gaze.

"So what is it like—modeling?"

Miriam looked up past his shoulder and shook her head lightly. "Busy. A lot of rushing around because there's a ton of people involved in a shoot or a show." She laughed, but it wasn't a pleasant laugh. "The work isn't so bad. It's how you get treated after a while."

"And how is that?"

"Like a thing—a centerpiece that gets pulled on, tweaked,

changed, and molded. Some girls love all the attention, but I felt like an object."

Jake heard despair in her voice. Despair and the same weariness he could see in her eyes. "So, why are you going back to it?"

Miriam gave a graceful shrug. "The money is good."

It wasn't hard to tell that she didn't like the work. He didn't want to accept that Miriam Spencer—a girl who never seemed to care what she wore, who used to wear her long brown hair tied back with a shoelace—had turned into this elegant woman who spoke easily of doing work she disliked merely because the money was good.

"Well, you've done it long enough—you must have quite a bit of it by now," he said sardonically. "Money that is."

She said nothing, only lowered her eyes—but not before Jake saw the flare of pain in them.

He felt like a heel. He had no right to judge her. Not when he himself often wished for better crops, for higher prices. Money was important to him, too.

He wondered what to say next. Wondered what he could say to bring some measure of amicability back to the conversation. Because he discovered, suddenly, that he wanted to know more about her, to find out what had happened to her.

As he watched her carefully sip her coffee, he felt a familiar stirring, an awakening of old feelings. She had been a friend—one of the first he had made here. Miriam had been the one who introduced him to other people, who included him in her circle, who made sure he was always socially comfortable. The friendship they shared had quickly changed and become more intense. Miriam was the first girl he had really loved.

And now, despite the complete change in her, and despite knowing she was leaving, he was feeling attracted to her again.

Fool that he was.

He wanted to leave as if to outrun his own feelings, but there was no polite way to do so. He had invited her here.

The door opened, and a woman called out a greeting to Peter, then walked over to their table.

"Hey, Jake, how are you doing?"

Jake looked up and met the smiling face of Donna Kurtz. "Doing good, Donna. How about you?"

"Busy. I just took a break from working at the church." She pulled at her paint-splattered T-shirt and flashed a crooked grin. "I thought you were going to come?"

He felt a rush of guilt. "I'm sorry. I forgot they're painting there today." He had forgotten that, in a rush of thinking he could do everything all at once, he'd volunteered to help. "I'll be right over."

He turned to Miriam, who was looking up at Donna with a wistful expression on her face. "Miriam, you remember Donna, don't you?"

Donna's mouth fell open as she finally recognized her old friend. Then she was leaning over, hugging Miriam hard. "My goodness," she said breathlessly. "Look at you, Miriam Spencer." Donna clutched Miriam's shoulders and shook her head in disbelief. "Have you ever changed! What are you doing back here? How come I never knew?"

"I just came back yesterday," Miriam replied.

"Really?" Donna glanced at Jake and then back at Miriam, her smile changing. "And you and Jake already met up with each other." The innuendo in her tone was unmistakable.

Jake figured he'd better dispel that notion immediately. "Miriam's car broke down not far from our place. I brought her into town to get it fixed."

Donna nodded, but her smirk showed that she didn't quite believe it. "It's just like old times, seeing you two together again."

Jake wished she would stop assuming a relationship

between them. It made him yearn for something that wasn't going to happen—Miriam's next stop was a real estate agency.

He glanced at his watch. He had other things to do, other obligations. If Denny was as fast as he said he could be, Miriam didn't have much longer to wait. Meanwhile, he could take care of some obligations. "I should go and help at the church," he said to Miriam, trying for a light tone. "Will you be okay here?"

"I have a few other errands to do."

Right. Real estate agent.

"Well, if you need anything, give me a call," he said.

"Sure."

She nodded as her eyes met his, then looked back at Donna. He felt dismissed and pushed his chair back.

"See you back at the church," he said, sending Donna a quick grin.

Donna nodded, then took over his place opposite Miriam.

He stopped at the till and paid for their coffees, then walked to his truck. As he got in, he saw Donna and Miriam through the window of the café. Donna was leaning forward, and Miriam's face held that same wistfulness he had seen before.

As he started the truck, he wondered what was going on behind those deep brown eyes of hers. Once, he would have been able to read the slightest nuance, but now she was as unreadable as a legal document.

He sighed and pulled away. As if he didn't have enough on his mind, now he had to go and complicate his life with this woman who was so different from the one he had once loved.

"I STILL CAN'T BELIEVE you're here." Donna rested her elbows on the red Formica tabletop, sipping her coffee, smiling across at her old friend. "It's been years and years. Too long."

Miriam acknowledged the comment with a nod and kept folding the napkin on the table in front of her. More guilt. "I know and I'm sorry." She lifted her eyes to Donna. "I don't think there's anything I can really say to excuse or brush it all away."

"I heard a few bits and pieces from Paula just after you left, but that's about it."

"Paula and I stayed out of touch, as well—" Miriam stopped, sorrow over their mutual friend thickening her throat. "Sorry." She looked down, blinking quickly. "I still can't get past her death. I just found out yesterday."

"It happened a while ago for me, but I can imagine it's a shock for you."

Miriam drew in a long breath to compose herself and then looked up at Donna. "After she got married, the relationship faded away."

"I imagine." Donna took another sip of coffee but held Miriam's gaze. "You know, when I saw you sitting here with Jake, it seemed just like old times."

"That's all they are, Donna—old times," Miriam said sharply. Donna's words struck too close to her own yearning.

Donna looked taken aback at Miriam's harsh tone. "I know that. It's just that we used to see you guys together all the time. That's all."

"I'm sorry, Donna. It's been so strange coming back here. Everything's changed so much."

Except that it was much the same, Miriam thought as she and Donna quietly sipped their coffee. Looking at Donna somehow made her realize what she had lost when she'd left. This place where she had grown up suddenly seemed secure, unchanging. Here were people who cared. She had been hugged more in the past two days than she had been in years. More people had asked with sincerity how she was doing.

For the past few years, she had been only a face, a body, an object. No one seemed to care about her soul, her heart.

"You've changed, too. I remember the first time your face showed up on the front cover of a magazine. It was the talk of the town."

"I'm sure it was."

"Oh, don't get all huffy with me. That's what Waylen is like. People are nosy, but they care." Donna grinned at her. "And now, you owe me. Big time." Donna tilted her head, her tone full of meaning. "You don't write, you don't phone. So, spill. What happened with you and Jake? What have you been doing? What is your life like? How's your mom?"

Despite the sorrow raised by Donna's questions, Miriam felt an easing of the tension that had gripped her since she'd come here. Easygoing, straightforward Donna never pulled any punches, never minced words. Never judged.

"My mom died six months ago." Again, Miriam stopped, swallowing hard.

"Oh, Miriam. I'm so sorry."

"I can't believe this," Miriam said, her voice shaky as Donna's hand squeezed hers tightly. "It's like each time I tell someone, I relive her death." She stopped, taking in a deep breath. "It was hard, but I think she was ready. She died quite peacefully."

"I'm so sorry," Donna said, stroking her arm with her other hand. "You've sure had enough to deal with."

Silence drifted up between them as Miriam wiped a fresh rivulet of tears, but this was the companionable silence of friends reestablishing their acquaintance.

"Sorry to dump on you like this. Hardly old home week, is it?"

"I'm your friend, Miriam." Donna smiled at her. "I'm supposed to help you, to listen to you."

"Thanks." Miriam felt another twinge of guilt that Donna should offer help and support when she herself had remained so distant.

"So, what is modeling like?" Donna asked, changing the

subject. "How do you feel when you walk out in front of all those people?"

Miriam didn't want to talk about modeling. She had fostered a foolish hope that when she came back here, she would be able to leave the other life behind her, if only for a while. But she had forgotten how intertwined lives are in a small town. Your news is my news.

"Lately, the majority of what I do is catalog work. I haven't done much runway work lately, and, to tell you the truth, it's boring."

"Boring?" Donna said in a tone of disbelief.

"Yes, Donna. Despite how glamorous it looks, it's dull, plodding work." She would have preferred to talk about her clothing retail business, but that was another failure in her life.

At least for now.

"Well, you still don't seem to have trouble keeping the weight off." Donna sighed, looking at Miriam. "I could never figure out how a girl so skinny could eat so much and not put on a pound."

"Always was a poor keeper. But enough about me," Miriam said suddenly. She didn't want to reexamine her life any more than she had to. She hadn't liked what she saw out east; she liked it even less here. "What about you? Married? Kids?"

"Yeah, I'm married. My last name is now Kurtz, and my husband, Keith, is an accountant. He moved here about eight years ago. We fell in love, and now I've got two kids. One in play school, the other in kindergarten. I'm busy with church, school. The usual." Donna smiled a self-deprecating smile. "My life must sound so dull."

Miriam shook her head, a feeling of melancholy gripping her. "It doesn't sound dull at all," she said quietly. "It sounds pretty good to me."

"Don't give me that." Donna held her gaze. "As if beneath every glamorous outfit you've ever worn beats a heart that deep down would love nothing more than to be at home baking chocolate chip cookies."

"I prefer macadamia nut, myself."

"See? A gourmet. You don't belong in this little hick town anymore."

Once, Miriam might have scoffed at the idea, but as she had traveled these past few years, she had been able to look at Waylen from a distance. "Waylen isn't as bad as you might think, Donna," she said.

"You sound serious."

"I am. The fashion life reads well in short magazine articles. But a good photographer can make anything—and I mean anything—look good," Miriam said with meaning. "I haven't met many sincere people in my business. They're either putting up with you because you might be useful to them, or they're sucking up to you because you are useful to them." She gave a shrug, knowing that she had already said too much. She hadn't come back here to show everyone how unsatisfied she was with her life.

"So, no one important in your life right now?"

"Nope. Footloose and fancy free." Her wry grin belied her casual tone. "My agent, Carl, is a darling, but he's married. I've not met Mr. Right yet." A lot of Mr. Wrongs, Lance being the poster child for bad relationships.

"I can't imagine that. I always thought you would be the one who would get married first," Donna said with a grin.

There it was again: the soft pain brought up by the innocent comment. The reminder of how close she and Jake had once been. How had she thought she could keep herself aloof from that?

"I'm sorry," Donna said, shaking her head. "Me and my big mouth." She sighed. "I don't know what happened between you and Jake. I don't suppose it's any of my business, but it was as much of a shock to me as anyone when he and Paula got married."

Miriam sensed the opening that Donna gave her but decided not to seize it. She had come to set the past to rest.

"Well, that's long over, and we've both changed a lot," Miriam said lightly. "Tell me about the rest of the people here. What's Linda doing? Still hoping to write that bestseller?"

They sat for another hour, chatting, talking, laughing. Miriam found herself drifting back into life in Waylen. It was familiar, and yet, listening to her friend talk easily about children and her husband, Miriam had a feeling that she had missed out on an important part of life. Her own life seemed shallow and frivolous by comparison.

Finally, Donna had to leave. "I should go. I've shucked my responsibilities long enough. Why don't you come back to the church with me? Sondra is there. I'd love to see the look on her face when you show up."

Miriam shook her head. She would have liked to come, but Jake was there, as well. It would be better if she kept her distance as much as possible. "I have a few other things to do. Thanks, though."

"You said you're staying around a while—we'll have to make sure to connect again. Otherwise, the church is having a picnic a week from this Sunday. You should come."

Miriam paused again, considering. Memories of other fun-filled days flashed through her mind. "That sounds good."

"Great. Well, keep in touch. And we'll see you on Sunday."

They left the restaurant, each going her separate way. Miriam watched Donna stroll down the street, waving at one person, stopping briefly to chat with another. For a moment, she wanted to go with Donna. She wanted to be a part of that community.

Don't be silly. You don't fit here anymore, she thought. She wondered if she should go to church on Sunday. If she wanted to risk the very stares and censure that Donna had hinted at.

She had enough self-doubts; she didn't need to pile on any more.

But she remembered other times in church, other times when she had felt peace, and joy, and love. She felt a yearning to experience that again, that healing, that feeling that someone did care about her, about her soul. That she was important to God.

She had strayed so far from that center of her life. She couldn't help but think of how easy it had been to drift away, to get caught up in the vacuousness of the fashion world. And she had been such a major part of it—dressing up, acting, being fussed over.

Seventeen years old, self-conscious, still smarting from Jake's defection. What girl wouldn't go a little crazy with all that attention, all those photographers telling her how beautiful she looked, all the admiration? But it was from people who saw her only as a face and figure.

Miriam spun around and strode away from the café, wishing she could as easily leave parts of her past behind.

Carl and his bright ideas, she thought. It would have been easier on her self-esteem and her conscience if she had just stayed out east and sold the farm from there. She never spent this much time noodling about might-have-beens. All her free time in the past few months had been taken up with bankers, phoning up suppliers to beg for extensions of credit, and phoning up debtors to beg for payment.

Trying not to feel too humiliated about how Lance, her ex-boyfriend, had abused her trust.

Her life seemed to be a series of men who didn't want to stay with her, be loyal to her. That's why it puzzled her that Jake could still tie her up in knots. He had only been the first of many men who didn't seem to need her in the long run.

She sped up and this time made it all the way to the real estate office. She pushed the door open and stepped inside.

Half an hour later, she was back on the street. The

papers were signed, and the machinery had been put into place. So easy to get rid of the largest part of her life. Her home.

Miriam emerged from the office and sighed, looking down the street. A few trucks drove by, a couple of cars. People greeted each other as they passed on the street. Everyone belonged here. They fit.

She walked down the street until she found an empty bench and, wiping the moisture off it, sat down. She called Denny's on her cell phone and arranged for them to bring her car downtown. Then, just to make a connection, she phoned Tilly. Maybe she needed some groceries.

"That would be wonderful, Miriam," Tilly said when she answered and Miriam offered. "I don't dare leave Fred. He is feeling so listless, I don't want to leave him alone."

"He's still not feeling well?"

"It seems so up and down. If he doesn't get better, I'll have to take him in to the doctor. But for now, all is well, and God is good. We still have each other and Jake and Taryn, and for that, we can be grateful, can't we?"

Yes, you can, thought Miriam.

"Now, what groceries do you want?" Miriam wrote down what Tilly told her. They chatted a bit more, and then Tilly said goodbye. It was like old times, Miriam thought with a smile as she closed the phone. Running errands, idle chats.

She missed it.

She was putting her phone and the list back in her purse when she saw a tall figure pausing at the traffic lights on the main street. Jake. Obviously done at church. Probably looking for her.

He was frowning. Miriam could see it from here. She swallowed down her quick response to him, frustrated with how easily old feelings came back. The light turned green, and he crossed the street. He walked along the street opposite her, then looked up and saw her. His step faltered, then, after a quick glance both ways, he jogged across the street toward her.

Visiting with Donna this morning had recreated the past. Now, once again, as Jake sauntered up to her, she felt the same foolish thrill she always did when she saw him. It didn't matter that just this morning she had seen him with mud on his face and pants; he still seemed to tower above her, to dominate the area around him.

"Hello," she said evenly. "You finished already?"

"They didn't need me after all. I had some other business to do."

"I'm picking up some groceries for Tilly."

"That's not necessary," Jake said abruptly. He shifted his weight and slipped his hands in the back pockets of his blue jeans. "I can get them."

Miriam felt dismissed. Though she wanted to fight it, she realized that putting her farm up for sale pulled her back from their lives, as well.

She busied herself looking through her purse, found the piece of paper on which she had written the list, and handed it to Jake. "Are you sure? I don't mind doing it."

"That's okay. Thanks anyhow." He forced a smile, as if to compensate for his brusque attitude, but Miriam wasn't fooled. She knew what Jake's sincere smile could do. And had he bestowed one on her, she wouldn't be standing here, seething over how easily he seemed to exempt her from his life.

She had hoped to visit with Tilly for a while, but she'd have to make time for that another day.

"Well, I guess I'll see you around." She was about to turn.

"Did you want me to give you a ride to Denny's?"

"That's not necessary," she said, mimicking his words of a few moments ago. "They said they would deliver the car to me."

"Okay. I'll see you around then." And he turned on his heel and walked across the street again.

Miriam watched him go, her emotions narrowing down to anger. She felt as if she had been judged and found wanting. As if Jake Steele were above reproach, she thought angrily.

By the time Denny brought her car to town, she was tired and glad to see him.

She followed him back to the office and paid for the repairs done on her car. Thankfully, she had enough to cover that bill.

Then, without anything more to do, she drove home, fighting her most unwelcome frustration with Jake's offhand attitude. His easy dismissal of her offer to help.

The road back was still wet from the rain of this morning, and the car was difficult to handle, but that didn't stop Miriam from going too fast. She fishtailed a couple of times, and after the second time, forced herself to slow down. The last thing she wanted was for Jake to have to rescue her. Again.

By the time she got home, she wasn't quite as angry as before. Instead, a peculiar hurt overlaid her earlier emotions. A painful realization that she didn't fit here anymore.

Well, it was a good thing she had realized that as soon as possible and hadn't pinned anything on this place.

She parked her car and walked back into the house.

Once inside, she hung her purse up on the hook at the front door, toed off her shoes and took a moment to take stock. Figure out what she had to do to make the house habitable.

Last night, all she had energy for was cleaning the refrigerator before she dared put her groceries in. Then washing the linens on her bed and getting that ready to sleep in.

This morning, it was a quick bowl of cereal eaten standing by the sink, then off to town.

Now, with the afternoon and the evening stretching,

empty, ahead of her, she couldn't put off the reality of her situation anymore.

The house was dusty, dirty, and needed a good cleaning if she was staying here for the next couple of weeks. And if she was selling it.

The real estate agent, Anita, had told her she could hire someone to clean up the house and liquidate the assets for a portion of the proceeds. But as Miriam looked around, taking in the worn and tattered couch, the scarred and painted-over table and chairs, she doubted she could even donate most of the furniture.

She wasn't sure what all the boxes in the basement held. Boxes her mother had packed up after Miriam was shipped off to her Uncle Dale and Aunt Bertha in Toronto.

But they would have to be dealt with as well.

Before she sold the property, the best she could do was to hire someone to cart it off to the landfill.

But she could make it habitable for the time she would be here.

She literally rolled up her sleeves and got to work.

First off, she emptied the kitchen cupboards, surprised at how much her mother had left behind, then filled a pail with warm soapy water and started washing them out.

She worked her way through the kitchen, wiping down the cupboards, the chairs and the table, then the floor. Thankfully, in all the time it was empty, mice hadn't taken up residence. Otherwise, she would have an entirely different problem to deal with.

As she cleaned, her hands busy, her mind wandered back to happier times in the house. Meals around the kitchen table, just her and her parents. Memories of sitting on her father's lap while he read a story Bible. Teased and tickled her, calling her Mims. The same nickname Jake always used.

She pushed thoughts of Jake aside, scrubbing the floor with a vengeance.

Her old bedroom had been emptied of anything that belonged to her. The only thing left was the bed she had slept in last night and the quilt her paternal grandmother, Nana Spencer, had made for her. Nana, a widow when Miriam was born, had passed away long ago, and Miriam knew virtually nothing about her mother's family. Edna never spoke of them.

The only family members she knew were Uncle Dale and Aunt Theresa in Toronto.

Where she'd been sent during her last year of high school. They didn't have any children, and while they were decent people, they simply tolerated her until Miriam's mother moved there as well.

Miriam often felt untethered because of the lack. No siblings. No aunts or uncles close by. No cousins. No extended family get-togethers.

That was why she clung too hard to Fred and Tilly and made them her family.

And Jake? Was he her family too?

Enough.

Get to work.

Six hours later, the house was as clean as she could get it. And she was tired and worn out.

All she managed for supper was scrambled eggs and toast, eaten on the worn couch in the living room. No television, so she scrolled through her phone.

Then, when weariness dragged at her and she couldn't keep her eyes open anymore, she made the trek upstairs to her bedroom. But before she turned to go inside, she paused, looking across the hall at the door of her mother's room. Her cleaning spree hadn't included this space. After her father died, this room was off-limits unless she was invited in. Forbidden.

But her mother was gone. And she was no longer the young girl who lived in fear of her mother's anger.

Her back stiffened, and lifting her chin, she twisted the knob and pushed the door open.

As she looked around, another flood of memories washed over her.

Sitting on the bed on her birthday as her father handed her birthday gifts. Her mother smiling. Then.

Times she was sick, and her father would let her sleep with them. He snored horribly, and she didn't get much sleep, but lying between him and her mother made her feel safe and loved.

Something that changed drastically after her father's death. At the time, she was a young girl, grieving herself, not understanding why her mother was so angry all the time.

Now that she was older, she understood somewhat better. And her mother's struggle to apologize before she died cleared away some of the pain of the distance her mother created between them. The criticism she levelled at everything Miriam did.

With a heavy sigh, she glanced around the room one more time, then left, closing the door on the memories.

For now.

SATURDAY DAWNED WARM AND BRIGHT, and after a quick breakfast, Miriam headed outside. Today, she was tackling the yard, so it didn't depress her so much each time she stepped outside.

She walked through the tangled lawn surrounding the house, past the overgrown flowerbeds, and through the metal arch her father had made and down the worn path to the large shop hulking behind the house.

The tractor it used to house had been gone long ago, as had the farm implements he used to farm their land.

She slowed her steps, looking up at the endless sky, something she never saw living in the city. Always blocked by high-rises and apartment blocks. But now she could see the sky from horizon to horizon. The fields that rolled away from the farm were brown, broken by lines of trees holding a whisper of green. Almost a mile away, she saw a cloud of dust roiling behind a tractor pulling an implement of sorts. Soon that field would be ready for planting.

Spring was here, and she could smell it in the air, hear it in the spiraling songs of the birds in the trees hugging the house, the willows edging the path toward her father's shop.

For a moment, nostalgia blended with a yearning for this place. Settled. Solid. Surrounded by land that had been passed down through her father's family. A heritage that she was about to end once it was sold.

Her heart twisted at the thought, but reality settled her uncertainty.

She had debts to pay and a business to salvage. Sentimentality didn't pay bills. Selling the farm would ease the crushing burden she had been carrying since she discovered how badly she'd been cheated.

With a shake of her head to settle her thoughts, she shoved her hands in the pockets of her linen pants and strode to the shop.

Stepping inside, despite her resolve, another wave of nostalgia washed over her at the pervasive scent of diesel and oil that seemed to have soaked into the very timbers of the building.

The smells brought other memories floating back. Her father helping her put the chain back on her old and worn bike for what felt like the twentieth time, patiently helping her. The time he worked with her here on her science fair project about bridges because her mother didn't want it done in the house. She remembered "helping" her father by handing him tools from the chest-high toolbox that still stood in one dark corner whenever he had to fix the tractor. Or the disc or the seed drill.

She had probably spent more time here with her father than with her mother in the house.

Though he'd been gone more years than he'd been in her life, sorrow clenched her midsection, and she pressed her hand to her mouth to keep it from escaping.

She took a breath and leaned against one of the workbenches, glancing around at all the other farm paraphernalia collected over the years. And anxiety now wiped away her momentary grief.

Yesterday, when she had signed the sales agreement, she hadn't realized the magnitude of her actions. She would have to have a farm sale to get rid of all these things.

The thought depressed her. She had been to enough farm sales as a young girl. She remembered how uncomfortable she had felt, poking and prying through other people's things, listening to disparaging comments made about some of the items offered for sale while the owner or owners stood by.

But imagining the contents of the house going up for sale bothered her less than the idea of seeing her father's tools lined up and auctioned off. Thankfully, she would probably be gone by the time that happened.

She wandered through the shop, taking mental stock, surprised to see so many tools still here. The lawn mower and garden tiller stood in their usual corner. Her father's table saw and drill press stood opposite, coated with a layer of greasy dust. Buckets and pails of bolts and nuts were lined up on shelves above the workbench. Mouse droppings were thick on the floor and an old leather carpenter pouch that had fallen off its hook had been fair game for them: it was full of holes.

For the rest, it was all intact.

With a mental shake, Miriam walked over to the lawn mower and pulled it away from the wall. She opened the gas tank and frowned. Empty, of course. And she knew there was no gas in the gas tank in the yard.

So much for mowing the lawn, she thought.

She could ride over to the Prins's farm and borrow some gas; her father had enough jerry cans she could carry it in.

But after meeting Jake in town, she was reluctant to go over there when he was around.

Monday, she could. Jake would probably be working in the fields then.

She pushed the lawn mower into its spot and walked back to the house, wondering how she was going to fill the rest of the day.

Chapter 5

$\mathcal{M}$iriam flipped down the visor in her car and checked her lipstick. She subconsciously ran her hand over her hair and glanced down at her clothes—black blazer over dark, narrow fitted pants. Conservative enough for church, she figured.

Yesterday, she had spent half the day trying to talk herself out of coming, but when she woke up this morning in her old house, it was as if the rituals and routines of the place echoed between its walls. So, she showered, dressed, and left.

She pulled the key out of the ignition and looked over at the large, older building, its spire stabbing the sky, pointing heavenward.

Maybe she should have just gone for a walk.

Standing here in the shadow of the church—the shadow of seventeen years of sermons, obligations, and Sunday School lessons—she felt as if she were looking at her recent life through another lens.

The parties, the late nights, the friends she had spent time with, the endless traveling from one exotic location to another, the many, many times she had thought she should visit her mother—and hadn't—all seemed so shallow now. She used to go but had stopped attending church when her co-workers teased her about it.

I was just young, she appealed to a distant God who was tied up with this church and her past. *I was finally free from obligations and a mother who never approved of anything I did.* She clutched her car keys tighter, their sharp ridges cutting into her palm, as if the pain would serve as penance for what she had done.

"I don't need this," she said to no one in particular, leaning back against the seat. "I didn't have to come today."

But she had.

She had come seeking peace, but instead, she was being faced with her past at every turn.

Miriam had never been a quitter, and she wasn't about to start now. She knew that people, once they found out she was back, would wonder why she hadn't come to church the way she always had when she and her mother had lived here.

So, straightening her shoulders, taking a deep breath, she stepped out of the car to finish this.

She walked slowly up the front walk to the church. A flat, wide sidewalk led to two sets of double doors.

Inside, a group of people stood in the foyer, chatting. They glanced at her, then smiled a polite smile before moving toward another set of stairs beside an elevator. Miriam didn't recognize them and was sure, from their reaction, that they didn't recognize her, either.

The doors behind her opened again, sending a shaft of light into the foyer. Miriam took a step away, making room for the people.

"Miriam," a sweet young voice called out, and Miriam spun around.

"Well, hello, Taryn." She smiled at the young girl who came running up to her. Taryn wore a yellow dress that flounced as she ran. Her hair was braided this time and tied up with two white ribbons. One ribbon, however, had come loose and was trailing down her front.

"You came to church." The statement was made without guile, and Miriam couldn't help but smile down at the adorable little girl. "Are you going to sit with us?"

"Maybe Miss Spencer wants to sit with someone else," Jake said to his daughter as he walked up to stand beside her.

Miriam reluctantly turned her gaze to him. His white collarless shirt was a bright contrast to his tanned complexion. His dark, wavy hair was brushed away from his face, bringing his features into stark relief.

Handsome as ever, thought Miriam with a stab of regret. His smoldering eyes, his full mouth. It was as if the man she had seen the other day, mud covering his face, his eyes sparkling—the man who had called her "Mims"—had been just a figment of her imagination.

Taryn looked up at her father, then back at Miriam, her eyes sad. "Do you want to sit with someone else?"

Miriam looked down at the little girl, her heart softening at the appeal in those eyes. Avoiding a reply, she squatted down and carefully retied the silk ribbon. "There," she said, giving the bow an extra tug. "I made it nice and tight. It won't come loose again."

Taryn lifted the bow, tucking her chin in and almost crossing her eyes to see it. "That looks nice. Daddy can't tie these very good. He says he has farmer hands." She grinned up at Miriam. "Can you fix the other one, too?"

Miriam didn't dare look at Jake. She sensed his displeasure, yet something stubborn in her nature made her bend over and quickly tie up the other bow, then fluff it out.

"Thanks, Miriam," Taryn said, unabashedly catching Miriam's hand in her own as Miriam straightened.

Fred and Tilly were coming toward her, walking slowly to accommodate Fred, Miriam surmised.

"Hi there, Miriam." Fred walked up to her and patted her on the shoulder. "So good to see you here."

Miriam smiled at the approval on his face. At least in Fred's eyes, she had gotten things right.

Tilly bustled up, greeting her with an enthusiastic hug. "I was so praying you would come today." She smiled, stroking Miriam's cheek.

Miriam felt another knot of emotion at the sincerity in Tilly's voice.

"I'm glad I came, too," she said softly, swallowing. She avoided looking at Jake but was conscious of him watching them, fully aware of his disapproval. It shouldn't have mattered, but Miriam felt it as strongly as she felt Tilly's love.

She wished she dared confront him, to try to explain, but her own emotions over Jake were too unstable, too vulnerable. She hated it, but it was a reality she had to accept. Once she was gone, it would go away, she figured. Once she was back at work, remaking her life.

"You can come with us, Miriam. Please sit with us." Taryn caught her hand. "Can she sit with us, Grandma?"

"Of course." Tilly smiled down at her granddaughter. "Will you, Miriam?"

Again, Miriam felt stuck. She knew Jake was not pleased yet couldn't find it in herself to pull her hand away from Taryn or to say no to her old neighbor.

"I guess I can."

"Goody." Taryn caught her father's hand in her other one and started pulling the two adults toward the stairs leading to the sanctuary. "C'mon, Grandma and Grandpa," she called over her shoulder. "We have to sit down."

Miriam felt the small, soft hand in hers, and something inside her melted. Suddenly, she didn't care what Jake thought, didn't care what anyone else thought. This precious little girl wanted Miriam to be with them, and it felt wonderful.

She tried not to read too much into the child's actions. Taryn seemed naturally precocious, but as they walked up the stairs, two adults joined by a young girl, Miriam's throat thickened.

She remembered walking precisely in the same formation with her parents. Her father on one side, her mother on the other, and little Miriam safe and secure in the middle, just like when she lay in bed with them.

The memory was so vivid that she bit her lip, fighting an unexpected sorrow, the stairs wavering in her vision. Ducking her head, she quickly wiped her eyes one-handed, hoping Jake wouldn't see.

And as she straightened, she felt Jake's eyes on her. She couldn't stop looking at him any more than she could stop Taryn's excited bouncing.

Once again, their eyes met and held. Once again, Miriam felt as if she were drifting toward him, unable to stop herself.

But Taryn gave them both another tug, and the moment was broken.

"Daddy has to get the bulletin," she announced to Miriam, swinging her hand. "You stay with me and Grandma and Grandpa."

Miriam looked down at the crooked part in the little girl's hair and resisted the urge to run her hand over Taryn's head, to bend over and gather this little girl in her arms.

Instead, she blinked once more and looked ahead to the sanctuary, already three-quarters full.

She knew the instant Jake returned. Out of the corner of her eye, she saw him take Taryn's other hand, almost felt his sidelong glance. She kept her eyes ahead, however, looking at the congregation, wondering where they would sit. A couple of people had already turned, then spun back around to whisper to a neighbor. This created a small ripple of movement among the people sitting in the back.

"Well, Miriam. Ready to face your past?" Jake's deep voice

seemed to mock her, but when she turned to challenge him, she saw his soft mouth curved up in a hint of a smile. "You're quite notorious, you know."

"Notorious?" she repeated, trying to inject a note of humor in her voice. "Disreputable notorious or distinguished notorious?"

"Probably a bit of both," Jake said, looking away.

"Let's go sit," Taryn urged, looking up first at Jake and then at Miriam. "They're going to start singing, and then everyone will look at us."

Judging from the number of backward glances they were getting, that was happening already, thought Miriam, looking down the long, carpeted aisle of the church.

Just another catwalk, she thought, and a different audience. She rolled her shoulders, lifted her chin, and reminded herself not to strut.

Tilly and Fred went on ahead, followed by Jake, Taryn, and Miriam. The aisle was wide enough for the three of them. She was thankful, however, that Tilly stopped halfway to the front.

They settled in the pew—Miriam, then Taryn, then Jake, and beside him, Tilly and Fred. Fred picked up the bulletin and started reading. Tilly leaned forward and started talking with the person ahead of them. Jake just crossed his arms and looked straight ahead.

Taryn sat between them, her hands folded demurely in her lap, her short legs sticking almost straight out in front of her. She tapped the toes of her shiny black shoes together, then looked up at Miriam with a huge grin. Miriam felt an answering tug of emotion. Taryn was so accepting, so open. Miriam didn't feel worthy of the obvious adoration that showed in the little girl's eyes.

The music from the piano stopped, then she struck the opening bars of a hymn. With a rustle and murmur, the congregation rose to sing.

Miriam took her cue from Jake and pulled a hymnal from the pew in front of her. The song sounded so familiar, but she couldn't place the title and didn't know where to find it. She tilted her head to see if the number was printed on the song board at the front of the church, but the board was no longer there.

She felt a hand on her arm and, turning, saw Jake's book tilted toward her; he was showing her the number. She nodded, a faint blush warming her cheeks when she saw the title. It *had* been a while since she had been in church, she thought with a measure of shame as she flipped through the pages. Too long, when she couldn't even find one of her one-time favorites in the hymnal.

The words sifted down through the past ten years of her life, through all her other experiences, the multitude of Sundays she had either been working or sleeping in because of a terribly late night. They pulled up old thoughts, old memories that Miriam had slowly buried under a deluge of new experiences that at first seemed exciting and now seemed cheap.

She stopped singing.

Once again, she felt as if she were a young girl standing beside her mother. A young girl whose every action was criticized and discussed at length within her hearing.

Miriam closed the hymnal and dropped it back into the holder, ignoring Jake's quick glance and Taryn's puzzled one. Instead, she stared straight ahead, waiting for the song to finish, hoping she would make it to the end of the service. She had thought she and her mother had laid these regrets to rest. Yet how quickly the feelings came back with the sound of an old hymn.

The song finally ended, and the minister strode up to the front and greeted them, his voice encouraging and hearty. He welcomed visitors, and Miriam noticed a couple of faces glance furtively at her. She ignored them.

Then everyone sat down, and Taryn looked questioningly up at her. Miriam smiled down, then looked away. She hoped she could just get through this service without making it too obvious to the little girl beside her that she suddenly wished she were anywhere else but here.

THE PIANO STRUCK up the first notes of the postlude, and Jake glanced at Miriam. She stood holding the pew, looking straight ahead, her short, dark hair shining under the overhead lights. She hadn't sung any of the songs and had sat through most of the service with her arms crossed tightly over her stomach, looking as if she'd sooner be anywhere else.

She turned her head and caught his eye, her expression composed. It was as if the woman who had wiped her eyes a while ago didn't even exist. He held her gaze, unable to stop his own reaction. This beautiful woman was a stranger, yet as he looked into her eyes and remembered her tears, he caught a glimpse of the girl he had once loved.

He turned away.

Taryn was chattering to Miriam behind him; Tilly was talking to someone else, signaling for him to go ahead. Jake ended up walking out alongside another farmer, discussing the weather and the condition of the pastures. He tried not to be aware of Tilly introducing Miriam to her friends, not to listen to Miriam's calm voice replying to breathless questions.

Sunday was always a quiet day, a true day of rest. And usually, he looked forward to it, but not today. He knew Tilly would invite her to lunch and didn't know if he wanted Miriam sitting across the table from him.

"Can you walk with me to the car, son?" Fred laid his hand on Jake's shoulder to get his attention.

Jake glanced down at his father. Fred's lips were edged

with a thin white line, and his complexion held a faintly grayish tinge.

"You okay, Dad?" Jake asked, alarmed at his father's ashen complexion.

"Just a little out of breath."

"I'm taking you to the hospital."

"No, Jake. Don't. The doctor told me this would happen occasionally. I want to get out of here. Fresh air is all I need."

"Okay," Jake said, taking his father's arm. But all the way to the car, he kept his eyes on the older man. It was hard not to look as if he was hovering. But by the time they reached the parking lot, some color had returned to Fred's cheeks.

At the car, Jake helped his father inside. Then he got in himself. "You're sure you're okay?" Jake asked one more time.

"I'm just tired." Fred laid his head back and then rolled it sideways to face Jake. He smiled and took a slow, deep breath. "And how are you? Are you okay?"

"Yes." Jake frowned, wondering what his father was getting at.

"Doesn't bother you to see her again?"

"Her?"

"Miriam. You used to like her quite a bit, didn't you?"

Jake raised his eyebrows, surprised at how perceptive his father was. "Yes, Dad. I did."

"And now? She's still single, I gather."

"She's also come to sell her farm and then go back east."

Jake glanced at Fred again, trying to gauge his reaction.

"You going to put an offer in on it?"

"I don't know. I really don't know." Jake knew he wouldn't be able to bluff his father. Fred knew the precise financial situation of the farm.

"It would be a shame to lose it."

"But I would be doing it with your money. I'm not a risk-taker."

"The price of cereal crops is edging up," Fred reassured

him. "Canola is looking really good. You'll make your money on the land. Eventually. And you'll have it as an asset. Sometimes you have to take risks, Jake…in various parts of your life."

Jake knew Fred alluded to more than just the farm but decided to leave it be.

"You might want to consider it. Have something to maintain, to pass on."

"I don't have a son, Dad," Jake said with a smile.

"That's okay, Jake. Neither did your mother and I." Fred returned Jake's smile. "And look what happened to us. God brought us you."

Jake felt a surge of tender warmth at his father's comment. "And I'm so glad he did."

Fred only nodded and then laid his head back, closing his eyes again. Jake could tell he wanted to go home, and he got out of the car to find his mother and Taryn.

Just as he did, he saw them with Miriam, walking over to the graveyard.

Jake watched, realizing what they were up to. Tilly had Miriam's arm tucked in hers and was talking, her head bobbing. Taryn skipped ahead of them, her braids bouncing with each step, her arms held out straight from her sides.

They walked directly to Paula's grave, and Taryn bent over to trace her mother's name. Running back to Miriam, she caught her arm and pulled her along.

From his vantage point, Jake couldn't read Miriam's expression. He wondered what she was thinking. Miriam and Paula had been friends for years, yet Paula had never seemed to have the same devotion to Miriam that Miriam had held for Paula. Of course, thought Jake, Paula always took care of Paula first.

Miriam stopped in front of the stone and clasped her hands in front of her, her head bent.

Jake felt a stab of guilt at the sight. Taryn and Tilly occasionally went to Paula's grave. He never did. When Paula had died, his sorrow had been tempered by a guilty measure of relief. Paula had been difficult to live with. During their marriage, she had hardly been around. Even after Taryn was born, Paula had managed to find all kinds of reasons to be gone. It was on one of her many trips away that she was killed.

The little group stood still for a moment, and Jake was surprised to see Miriam reach up to palm her cheeks.

Taryn, never able to stay still too long, started running to other stones. Tilly and Miriam tarried a moment, moved on, then stopped again. Jake guessed they were looking at her father's grave.

Tilly put an arm around Miriam's shoulder, and for a moment, Jake felt sorry for Miriam. He had stood beside the grave of a beloved foster father. He knew what it was like to lose a loved one. Miriam had no parents at all now. Her father was buried here and her mother out east.

At least he still had parents whom he loved.

For a moment, Jake wondered about his own mother. Wondered why she gave them up when she did. And did it matter? She was gone. That. Much hew and Simon knew.

Taryn saw him and came running over. "We saw my mommy's grave," she called out cheerfully. Tilly looked up and saw him, then said something to Miriam, who nodded and then left.

As Tilly walked across the parking lot, she waved at a few people, called out greetings to others. Then she saw that Jake and Fred waited and hurried her pace.

"Sorry," she said, puffing as she opened the back door of the car for Taryn. "Miriam wanted to visit the graveyard."

"She was sad again," said Taryn, scrambling into the back seat.

"Seat belt," warned Jake as she settled in.

"That poor girl. I'm glad she agreed to come over for

lunch," Tilly said, cinching her own belt. "She can seem so strong, but inside, she's hurting. She used to be so strong in her faith—I just pray she finds some peace here."

Jake started the car, his eyes on Miriam, who now walked back to her car, alone. For a moment, he, too, prayed for her.

Chapter 6

"So, you went to your aunt and uncle's place in Toronto, and then what?" Tilly asked Miriam as they cleared the table of dishes. Lunch was over, and Jake and Taryn were playing a game on one corner of the large oak table. Fred was lying down in his bedroom.

Miriam watched Taryn for a moment, remembering the many times she had sat in the same place Taryn now did, playing a game with Fred or Tilly, and later on, Jake. The sun poured in through the same flowered curtains. On the wall above the table ticked the same blue clock. The figurines in the window were the same as she remembered, and the sets of salt and pepper shakers still sat on the shelf that hung on one end of the wooden cupboard. It was home to her.

Miriam turned back to Tilly. "I stayed with them until my mom moved to Toronto. Then we found our own place. I finished high school, and shortly after I turned eighteen, I was scouted by a modeling agency."

"I never understood why your mother made you move there," Tilly said.

Miriam never knew for sure, but she had her suspicions. Her mother's reason was less transparent. She claimed she was moving anyway, to be closer to family. Miriam's agreement with the plan had as much to do with Jake as it did with not wanting to fight with her mother. The fact that he had pushed her away. Rejected her. Her broken heart had no energy to say no to her mother when she told Miriam they were moving.

"And what did your mother think of you becoming a model?"

Miriam drew in a slow breath, reliving the roller-coaster events of her life at that time. "At the end of my high school year, she suffered a debilitating stroke and needed extra care. Which meant I couldn't work full time. I found a job in a restaurant downtown. And that's where I got so-called discovered." She still remembered the misgivings she'd felt when her first agent, Darryl, had approached her with his business card and promises of money. "I turned Darryl down initially. I didn't believe what he was selling. But Mom encouraged me to at least check it out. So, I researched and found out that he was reputable. I went to see him, got some head shots done. Got a job right away and my life changed." She gave Tilly a wry smile as she set the bowls she had gathered onto the counter. "Thankfully, modeling gave me enough money to take care of Mom and keep us in our apartment. And thankfully, I had a good agent who took care of me. Got me some really great jobs."

"You never thought to move back here?"

"No. It would have been too difficult."

She declined to tell Tilly that the biggest part of that difficulty was finding out about Jake marrying Paula.

"I imagine you travelled a lot with that job. Where did you go?"

Miriam shrugged. "It wasn't so glamorous to start with. I did some catalog work, built up a portfolio, and from there, it was runway work. Italy. France. New York."

"That sounds so amazing to see such incredible places."

Miriam just nodded. She didn't want to admit that she couldn't remember a lot of those years. One place melded into another in her mind—planes, hotels; up early to catch good light, up late to catch the best party. Then doing it all over again the next day or week.

"Well, I'm glad you're back here. We've missed you." Tilly gathered up the rest of the pots and took them to the counter.

"Why did you miss her?" Taryn interrupted, looking up from her game.

"Because she was a good friend. She used to come over here all the time," Tilly replied, turning to her granddaughter.

Miriam fended off another attack of guilt at her lack of communication with Tilly and Fred. Mind you, Miriam told her mother very little either. She figured it would be better for Edna if she didn't know all the details of Miriam's life. The years she had spent traveling had left her rootless, living a life that had few adults in it to call her to account for what she had been doing. There was no voice of reason in her life, no guidance. Her mother could barely speak, let alone counsel her. Her agent was just there to find her work.

She realized now how important even a quiet word of caution or chastisement would have been at that time in her life.

"What's the matter, dear? You look troubled." Tilly laid her hand on Miriam's arm.

She shook her head and curved her lips into a smile. "I'm fine."

"I win, Daddy. I win," Taryn crowed. She gathered up the pieces of the game, then leaned her elbows on the table and looked at Miriam. "You want to play with me, Miriam?"

Miriam smiled at her as she picked up the cups from the table. "I should help your grandmother with the dishes."

"Oh, nonsense. You go and play with her. It takes nothing to load up this dishwasher." Tilly took the cups from Miriam.

Jake was still sitting at the table, leaning back in his chair, watching her through lowered eyes.

"I'll be blue, you can be red," Taryn suggested, handing Miriam a playing piece. "You know how to play Snakes and Ladders?"

"I think so," Miriam said, smiling.

Taryn grinned back. "I can start, okay?"

"Fine by me." Miriam settled beside her, directly across from Jake. She chanced a glance up at him, lifting her chin as if to say, *What is your problem?* Throughout dinner, she had felt as if he'd been watching, measuring. At first, it had made her feel uncomfortable; now it was getting annoying. He tilted his head a bit, as if to see her from another angle, then dropped his chair with a *thunk* on the floor.

"I SHOULD GO and check the cows." His voice was terse.

"I have to shake the dice and then count," Taryn explained to Miriam, ignoring her father.

"Miriam, did you put that pot in the sink?" Tilly asked, looking up from the dishwasher. "I thought I had rinsed it out."

"It's in the dishwasher," she replied, feeling a bit sorry for Jake. No one seemed to have heard what he said. She was about to ask him about the cows when Taryn poked her in the arm.

"Miriam, it's your turn."

"Taryn," Jake said, his tone hard. "Don't be rude."

Taryn looked down, immediately contrite. "Sorry, Daddy."

Jake looked around the kitchen, blew out a sigh, and left.

Miriam watched him go, unable to keep her eyes off him. They hadn't spoken more than two words to each other since he had opened the meal with prayer. She had caught him looking at her during the meal but had tried to act casually. It was difficult. She had thought their time spent in town might have eased away any awkwardness. But she had been wrong. He sat across the table as disapprovingly as he had the first day she had come here.

She yearned to fix what hovered between them, even though, if she thought about it logically, it seemed pointless. She wouldn't be staying, and once she was gone, she wouldn't be returning.

She turned back to the game and Taryn.

Twenty minutes later, with the dishwasher humming in the background and Tilly sitting at the table reading some material she had gotten from church, Miriam figured it was time she left.

"No. Stay a little longer," Taryn said. "We can play another game."

"We've already played four games," Miriam said with a smile, getting up from the table. She laid a finger on Taryn's nose and walked over to Tilly, dropping her hand on her shoulder. "Thanks for dinner. I really appreciate it."

"It was nice to have you." Tilly got up and pulled Miriam close. "It has been too long." She held Miriam by the shoulders, looking at her with her penetrating blue eyes. "You won't let that happen again, will you?"

Miriam bit her lip and shook her head. "No. I'm sorry." Apologies again, she thought. "Please give my regards to Uncle Fred for me."

"I will. I'll stop by sometime this week, when Fred's a little better. Are you going to be around?"

"For a while yet."

"Good. We'll have time to catch up." Smiling, Tilly walked with Miriam to the porch.

Miriam pulled her coat off the hanger and turned once more to Tilly, her heart softening at the sight of the older woman standing in the doorway the way she had so many times when Miriam had come over as a girl. "Thanks for having me over," she said quietly. "It meant a lot to me."

"I'm glad. You come again."

Taryn had followed them and now leaned against Tilly. Tilly absently stroked the little girl's head, and once again, Miriam felt a clutch of envy. Taryn didn't know how fortunate she was, she thought—to be loved so unconditionally by so many people.

Miriam tossed them a quick wave and then, turning, left. She hurried down the sidewalk, wrapping her coat around her against the cool wind that had sprung up.

She pulled her car keys out of her purse and was about to press the remote starter when she heard her name being called.

Stopping, she lifted her head to see where the voice came from, then saw Jake come striding across the yard, his hands in the pockets of his denim jacket, collar pulled up against the chill.

Miriam watched him approach, allowing herself a moment to appreciate his height and the easy way he carried himself. Jake had always had a quiet maturity, a steadiness that had appealed to her own young, flighty nature. And once she got to know him, he had a surprising vulnerability. But the Jake Steele she'd known was but a boy compared to the man who now marched toward her. This man was harder, more reserved. Each time their eyes met, it was as if he were appraising her. She never felt as if she measured up to whatever he was comparing her to.

She wondered what he wanted to say to her now. Throughout the meal, he had been quiet, watching her with those deep brown eyes that at one time had melted her heart but now seemed as uncompromising as the Ten Commandments she had heard this morning.

"How are the cows?" she asked as he came closer. She was determined to treat him the same way she would treat any man she had just met—to be chatty and interested in what he was doing but keep her emotions firmly intact. Ten years was long enough to move on, and it was time she did.

He stopped beside her, his shoulders hunched against the wind. "They're good. I'm moving them out to pasture in a few days."

"Enough grass already?"

"It's a bit nip and tuck. I only have enough hay to feed them for another week."

"That's too bad. I thought the rain the other night would have helped with the pastures."

She was doing an admirable job of slipping back into her "country" persona. Next thing, she'd be asking him how many acres of canola he was going to plant and what kind of weed spray he was going to use.

She was also surprised he was playing along. Probably just postponing what he had to say.

She fiddled with her key chain, trying to think of something casual to fill the silence.

"Miriam."

Jake spoke her name quietly, almost in entreaty. Miriam couldn't stop looking up at him, couldn't stop her heart from pounding. To her shame, hearing him speak her name made her feel as breathless as a young girl in the throes of her first crush.

Which Jake had been.

He was standing quite close to her, his hands in the pockets of his coat, holding it open. Their eyes met, and Miriam forced herself to try to breathe normally at the connection. "Yes?" she asked.

"I, uh, was wondering if you…" He paused again, and Miriam felt a foolish lift of her heart. He sounded the way he had the first time he'd asked her out on a date.

Don't be utterly ridiculous, Miriam reminded herself. *You are both older and wiser. He's a father, a widower who pushed you away.*

She forced herself to keep silent, to wait to see what he wanted.

Jake shoved his hand through his hair and held her gaze, his own steady, relentless.

"How long did you say you were going to be here?" he asked.

"I'm staying until next week Tuesday. Then I have to leave."

He nodded again, biting his lower lip. He wanted to say something else to her, she sensed.

"I, uh, don't know how to say this," he began. "But I get a real feeling that Taryn is becoming quite attached to you."

Miriam shrugged the notion off. "I'm just a novelty in her life. That's all."

"I hope so. I don't want her to be hurt."

Miriam felt his words as much as heard them. "I understand exactly what you are getting at, Jake," she replied, her anger rising. "I can't imagine what you think I would do to her."

Jake looked down, digging the toe of his boot in the ground, then glanced back up at her. "Taryn forms attachments very quickly. After Paula died, I made the mistake of bringing a girlfriend home to meet her. When we split up, Taryn was more brokenhearted than either me or the girlfriend. I don't want to see that happen to her again."

"I'm hardly a girlfriend, Jake," she said, the words sounding harsh even to her.

"That's true. I'm sorry if you misunderstood me, but I have to take care of her."

Miriam unclenched her fists and forced herself to relax. "I realize that, Jake."

Silence followed her comment.

Then Jake took a step back. "Well, I better let you go then." He turned and walked away, his head bent to the wind.

Miriam clutched her own coat closer to her, swallowing

down resentment over her life situation and anger over Jake's. He was only doing what he had to. He was taking care of his family first. She couldn't blame him for that.

But it still hurt.

In Jake's life, Taryn was first.

She acknowledged the rightness of it even as she felt an alarming jealousy that this girl was now the most important person to Jake.

Even if there was a slight chance, even just a hint, that Jake was interested in her, Miriam knew that she wasn't a suitable person to be Taryn's mother. Between her lifestyle and this one was a rift that couldn't be crossed. Her life was just a wasteland of broken dreams and promises. She really didn't have anything to give anyone. She wouldn't know how to be a mother, how to be a wife. The reality was that she was broke, out of work. She had a debt load that overwhelmed and frightened her any time she thought about it. Even with the work Carl promised, it would take a long time to repay.

She was no longer an asset to a man, to someone like Jake. She would be more of a liability in many ways.

Miriam got into her car, put it into gear, and backed out of the driveway, wondering how she was going to last her allotted time here.

ON MONDAY AFTERNOON, Miriam pulled into Fred and Tilly's driveway. From what she could see, the big tractor Jake used for field work was gone. Probably out cultivating. Which meant he would be gone most of the day.

Safe, she figured. She needed some gas to fill up her lawn mower, and there was none at her place. She had spent most of the day sorting through the stuff she and her mother had packed up and moved to the basement. After her "talk" with

Jake, she had been so upset that she had had to keep busy, to keep her hands and mind occupied.

After about seven trips to the community landfill, she had substantially reduced the number of boxes left over. What was left could be put up for sale, and most of those boxes, she had moved to the shop.

So, now the outside needed to be cleaned up. Anita, the real estate agent, had said she would be coming either today or tomorrow to take a picture, and Miriam figured she might as well make it look as good as possible. Which meant mowing the lawn and cleaning out the overgrown flower beds.

Stepping out of the car, she looked around the yard. Beyond the huge barn, she could hear cows bellowing. She wondered if something was wrong.

Curious, she walked past the barn and to the corrals beyond. Climbing up on the fence, she saw the herd of cows hanging around the two huge metal feeders—they were empty.

Cows probably need to get fed, she thought, stepping down. She walked back to the house and knocked on the door. No answer. Puzzled, she pushed open the door and put her head in.

"Hello, anybody home?"

"I'm in the living room, Miriam," Tilly called out. Miriam stepped inside, kicked her shoes off, and walked in.

Tilly was sitting on the recliner, reading. She looked up when Miriam came in. "Hello, dear. So good to see you again." She put the footrest down and got up. "Come in, sit down."

"I can't stay long. I was just wondering if I could get some gas. I need to mow that lawn."

"Oh, I'm sure you can. Do you remember which tank is diesel and which one is regular?" Tilly asked with a frown. "I know I don't."

"I can probably figure it out." Miriam glanced around. "Where are Fred and Taryn?"

"Taryn is at play school, and Fred is sleeping. He took a bad spell right after Jake left. Do you want something to drink?"

"No. I should get back to the house. It looks like there's a rain shower coming, and I want to get the lawn mowed before that. I'll probably stop by tomorrow."

"You do that, dear."

"What's wrong with the cows? They're sure making a lot of noise. Are they hungry?"

Tilly's hand flew to her mouth. "Oh, no. Fred was supposed to feed the cows this morning. Jake told him not to, that they could wait, but Fred was insistent. Now he won't be able to." She shook her head. "I guess they'll have to wait until Jake comes home. And he'll be so tired."

Miriam hesitated. It was none of her business what happened to Jake's cows. Yet, she could see how genuinely distressed Tilly was.

Tilly got up and put her book down. "I'll just have to feed them myself. I'll have to phone the school to tell them I'll be late picking up Taryn."

Miriam had to smile at the thought of Tilly sitting in a tractor, wearing her ever-present skirt and blouse.

"Don't be silly," she said suddenly. "I remember helping Jake feed the cows. I can do it."

"No, dear. You don't have to do that. You're here for a holiday."

"Feeding the cows is hardly a huge chore," Miriam said with a laugh. "It will be a nice break for me."

"Are you sure?"

Miriam could see obvious relief on Tilly's face, and nodded. "Think of it as payment for the gas I have to borrow."

"Hardly seems fair. But if you don't mind, it will work out

well for me. I have to pick up Taryn in half an hour, and I know Fred can't do it. Not now."

"Then that settles it. We don't want her waiting for you." Miriam patted Tilly on the shoulder. "You just sit down and take it easy. I'll get those cows fed."

AN HOUR LATER, Miriam jumped out of the gate and closed it behind her. The tractor with the bale forks had no cab, and she was still picking hay out of her hair and wiping dust out of her eyes. She figured she looked a fright but didn't care. It was fun driving the tractor, dumping the huge round bales into the feeder, and trying to avoid running over cows or calves. After depositing the last bale, she had backed up and simply sat and watched the calves racing around, their tails up in the air, then stopping suddenly and coming back to check out who this strange person was.

She still had to smile, thinking of how clean and fresh they looked compared to the cows. She had forgotten how cute they could be and how much fun they were to watch. For a moment, she was the Miriam of old, helping Jake with his chores, hoping her mother wouldn't find out.

She walked back to the tractor and climbed on, put it in gear, and then drove it to where it had originally been parked. She had to stand up to turn the wheel; the steering was tight, and the front-end loader made it that much more difficult to maneuver.

But she'd done it, she thought proudly as she shut off the roaring engine.

She blinked some more and then climbed off. Before she'd fed the cows, she had filled her jerry can with gas, and Tilly had now left to pick up Taryn. Miriam could leave right away.

With a smile, she turned—and almost ran smack into Jake.

Miriam swallowed and took a step back. "Hello," she said

quietly, wiping her hands on her pants. "I fed your cows for you."

"I see that," he replied, not moving.

"I came to get gas for my lawn mower, so I figured I would do it. Tilly seemed quite worried about them." Miriam flashed him a self-conscious smile.

"I was just coming home to do it."

He sounded defensive, and Miriam felt that once again, she had done the wrong thing.

"Whatever," she said, dismissing his comment. She went to walk past him, and as she did, he caught her arm.

She turned to him and subconsciously pulled her arm back.

"Sorry," he said, dropping his hand. "I just wanted to say thanks. I really appreciate the help."

Miriam sensed a discord between them that came up with each encounter. She knew it had as much to do with their past as their present, but she didn't know how to work through it.

Or even if she wanted to. What would it accomplish?

"You're welcome," she said. Then she turned and left.

But as she got into her car, she glanced over to see Jake watching her.

Back at home, Miriam threw herself back into her work. She mowed the lawn, trimmed the hedge, pruned the apple trees; and when the shower she'd talked of came, she found other things to do.

The next morning, the sun was shining and birds trilled their songs, calling her out.

She had a few other things to do and then planned to go over to Fred and Tilly's. It was beautiful weather, so she could probably avoid Jake. Most likely, he was out in the field again.

She had spent most of last night and part of this morning sorting through the rest of the boxes in the basement, deciding what she wanted to keep and what to throw out.

She managed to put aside about two boxes' worth of

keepsakes and mementos for herself—the photo albums, a few old books and records, a set of baby booties her mother had saved.

Miriam turned her head to look out the living room window, smiling at the sight of the lawn. It was a neatly clipped sweep of green, broken by a single maple tree dominating the front yard. Tall aspen trees, misted with spring green, surrounded and protected it. Beyond them a double row of spruce trees stood guard, sheltering the yard on all sides from wind.

Outside had always been Miriam's sanctuary. Outside was where she went to get away from her mother and her constant demands.

Miriam pushed herself off the couch and got up. She needed to get away from the house…and the memories.

She found her jacket, zipped it up, and stepped outside with the same sense of freedom she had felt as a young girl whenever she managed to get away.

Inhaling the warm scent of spring, she started walking briskly down the driveway. She didn't have any destination in mind, just a desire to get away from the cobwebs, the dust, and the past.

The driveway was shielded by double rows of trees, and by the time Miriam saw the road, she felt her burdens slough off her. As she walked down the familiar route, she felt the peace that had always eluded her in the house now float down over her weary soul.

The land was open here, rolling and welcoming. She let her eyes drift over the fields, the trees. Memories of her life in New York became overlaid with the combed-looking fields that had already been cultivated, the pastures that were greening up. The soft, spring wind sifted through the trees alongside the road, and from the power line above came the sweet song of a sparrow.

Spring in the country.

Miriam felt a gentle stirring of her heart as the atmosphere surrounded her, drawing out happy memories, moments of utter abandon and freedom.

How often had she and her friends sat, hunkered over the ditches, floating sticks and leaves in the spring runoff? How often had they taken her horse and, doubling up, ridden off in whichever direction the day took them?

Paula's face came to her mind, and Miriam bit back a sudden cry. Paula, her good friend. Paula, who had listened to Miriam's adolescent complaints about her looks. Paula, who had been her confidante when Miriam had discovered her growing love for Jake Steele, the boy so many girls liked. Paula, who had ended up with the prize, after all.

Now Paula was dead. Sorrow tightened Miriam's throat, pressed on her heart.

Miriam couldn't stop the tears drifting down her cheeks, cooled by the spring breeze. She couldn't help but remember the sight of Taryn pointing out her own mother's gravestone. Seeing Paula's name etched in the granite slab had made her death so definite, so real.

She wondered if Paula and Jake had been happy for those few years they had been together. She wondered if Jake mourned her very much.

Once again, jealousy gripped her.

Shaking her head, she tried to pull herself away from these maudlin thoughts. "Just enjoy the day," she said aloud. "Just enjoy the day."

A thicket of spruce and aspen trees beckoned, and as she walked through the moldering undergrowth, the spicy scent of freshly opened aspen leaves teased her nose. Willow branches caught at her, but she finally found the game trail that led her deeper into the bush.

And there it was, high up in the boughs of a large pine tree—the remnants of her old tree house. A few boards speckled with lichen and moss hung from a couple of nails, and the platform was still in place. On the tree beside her were nailed the single boards that provided a shaky ladder to her old retreat.

She smiled, remembering how many fantasies had been spun here. When she was older, she and Paula had come here...until Paula declared herself "too big" for games like this.

Then when she and Jake started dating, this fort had become a haven for them. Here, they could sit and talk of the future, make plans, dream.

Miriam smiled lightly, then turned away. It seemed memories of her past romance with Jake would come to her no matter what she did or where she went.

She walked back the way she had come and returned to the road. Once there, she set out for nowhere in particular. She just wanted to walk and to enjoy the fact that today she had no other obligations, no concerns.

As she walked, she looked around, seeing the spread of the land, the various hues of green that told her summer was almost here. Soon the cows would be out on pasture.

"And all the trees of the field will clap their hands..." The quote came to her lips as she paused, looking out over the land.

She stood, looking out and smiling and for the first time since she had come, felt a measure of peace. A soft breeze swirled around her like a benediction, rustling through the leaves of the trees above as if they were indeed clapping their hands.

There was joy in the air, and Miriam pulled it to herself and let it flow through her.

She tried to memorize each line of trees, each glade, the flow of the fields, the pastures, the farmyards she saw, and the barns and grain bins that filled them. This was where she had come from. She wanted to remember this moment, this very place. In future, when she was stuck in the oppressive heat of summer in New York, when she sweltered outside or shivered in air-conditioned cool inside, she would return to this place in her mind and know that somewhere life simply flowed instead of jerking and jumping around.

Miriam hadn't prayed in years, but now the words came to her lips unbidden. "Thank you, Lord," she whispered. "Thanks for this moment, for this part of the world."

She waited a moment, as if to acknowledge a certain holiness to the moment.

Then she began walking again.

She had walked for about fifteen minutes when she heard a car coming up behind her, heading toward town. She moved to the side of the road, hoping it would slow down. The road was still wet in spots, and she stood a good chance of getting splashed.

The car slowed, all right, and then came to a complete halt, the engine running. Miriam turned to see the window of the car slide down, Tilly looking strained. Fred was on the seat beside her, Taryn in the back.

"Hello, Miriam," she called out. "I tried to text Jake, but I'm taking Fred to the doctor. He fell when he got out of bed this morning, he was feeling so weak."

"Oh, no. Anything broken?" Alarm sang through her.

"Nothing broken. Just not feeling good."

Miriam couldn't help the fear growing in her chest. "Then you better get going," she said, glancing back to see Taryn sitting in the back seat, looking glum.

Tilly caught the direction of her gaze. "Jake was gone. Otherwise, I would have asked him to take Taryn. I need to take her with me."

Taryn leaned forward, a frown puckering her forehead. "I can't go to play school 'cause there's not play school today."

Today, Taryn wore blue jeans and a pink wind-breaker. Her hair was pulled back in a ponytail high up on her head, tied up with a matching pink ribbon. She looked adorable.

Tilly paused, frowning, glancing sidelong at Taryn, then back up at Miriam, beckoning to her to come closer. Tilly lowered her voice. "I know you're on a holiday, but I was wondering if you would be willing to take Taryn for the day."

"Please," Taryn pleaded, her hands curled into fists pressed under her chin. "Please let me come to your place."

Jake's admonition of the other day roiled through her mind.

"It would really help me out a lot," Tilly said.

Miriam looked down at Tilly, noting the wrinkles around her face. Yes, Tilly had grown older while Miriam had been gone. She looked tired and care-worn.

She bit her lip, remembering countless times she had sat in Tilly's kitchen, eating cookies and talking. Countless times she had complained to Tilly about her mother's unfair treatment. Hugs and kisses she had received from this dear woman who was as much of a mother to her as she had been to Jake. Helping her out now would be but a drop of kindness compared to the gallons of love Tilly had given her.

Jake wasn't here, and Tilly and Fred needed her.

"Of course," Miriam said, laying her hand on Tilly's shoulder and squeezing lightly. "I'll take her."

"Thank you so much," Tilly breathed, and as Miriam saw some of the strain leave Tilly's face, she knew she had done the right thing. She would just have to take her chances with Jake.

"Oh, goody, goody." With quick movements, Taryn unclipped her seat belt and jumped out of the car.

"You behave, now," Tilly said with a warning frown. Of course, Taryn nodded. She turned back to Miriam. "Thanks again, my dear. You've really helped me out a lot." Tilly smiled with relief, put the car in gear, then paused. "I don't know how long I'm going to be, but if I'm not home by suppertime, can I ask another favor of you?"

"Anything, Tilly," Miriam said with heartfelt sincerity.

"Jake is going to be working your fields sometime today, and I usually bring him supper so he can keep going. If I don't come back on time, I made a casserole for him. Can you see that he gets it?"

Miriam felt her heart slow at the thought of seeing the very man she hoped to avoid.

"I'll probably be home," Tilly said, acknowledging her hesitation. "But just in case."

"If you're not around, I'll see that he gets something to eat." Miriam shrugged fatalistically. *What would be would be.* "You just get Fred taken care of."

"Thanks again, Miriam." Tilly smiled at Taryn, then back at Miriam and with a wave, drove away, dust billowing up behind her.

Miriam and Taryn stood on the road, waving back as the cloud receded farther and farther, until it disappeared around a curve.

Miriam felt Taryn slip her hand into hers. She couldn't stop her own from tightening around the smaller one as she looked down at Jake's daughter. For a moment, she indulged in a dangerous "what if."

What if...she and Jake had stayed together? What if...this precious child had been hers and Jake's?

"Do you want to keep walking?" Taryn asked, grinning up at her, swinging her hand.

"I think we should go back to the farm."

"But I like walking."

"Then let's keep going. But only a little while longer." Miriam gently eased her hand out of Taryn's. She felt uneasy pulling back from Taryn's obvious affection but knew it was better if she didn't allow this young child to get too attached to her.

Just as Jake had warned.

Chapter 7

"*My* daddy is workin' on the tractor today, and then he has to move the cows." Taryn hopped across a puddle and flashed a grin at Miriam. "He's gonna be busy, he told me. But when he's all done, we're going to go to the city and buy me some pretty gloves. He promised me."

"You really love your daddy, don't you?" Miriam asked as she strolled along, hands in her pockets. She knew she shouldn't pry, but some part of her wanted to know more about Jake and his relationship with his daughter.

"I love my daddy the bestest. I loved my mommy, too, but she died," Taryn stated in a matter-of-fact voice. "My friend Suzy Adams has two mommies and two daddies."

"That's a lot of mommies and daddies," Miriam said with a shake of her head, wondering how often poor Suzy Adams was shunted from place to place.

"I just want one mommy," Taryn said, as if this were the most reasonable request in the world.

Miriam instinctively knew she had to change the subject and, at the same time, keep Taryn entertained. "Do you want to make a water wheel?" she asked, scanning the area for some cattails. She saw some on the other side of the road, their brown heads tilting slightly in the breeze.

"What's a water wheel?"

"You make it out of two cattail stems." Grinning, Miriam walked over to the cattails and reached into her back pocket for a pocketknife.

"Oops," she said, laughing and looking sheepishly back at Taryn. "I don't have a knife, so I can't make one." Funny that she would do that, she thought. "I forgot I don't carry one anymore."

"That's okay. My daddy always has a pocketknife. It has a tweezer and a scissor. It's a red pocketknife and has J.S. on it. That means Jake Steele. He told me that. He got it as a present from someone special—not from my mommy though." Taryn chattered on as she bent over to look at a rock, poking it with one finger.

Miriam's feet slowed, a spark kindling within her. After all these years, Jake still had the pocketknife she had given him, the one she had saved up her meager allowance for. She allowed herself a moment of wondering why.

Don't be silly, girl. Miriam pulled her thoughts up short. *He's always been careful with the things he has, that's all.*

"We should probably go back. It's quite some way to walk yet," she said to Taryn, who now had three rocks clutched in her hands.

Though Miriam didn't encourage her, Taryn chattered while they walked, bringing Miriam up to date on what was happening in her life, her father's life, and Tilly and Fred's lives. It was a bittersweet pleasure to Miriam to hear about Jake—how much he was at home, how often he slept in the recliner in the evening, how he liked to read Taryn stories.

They had come to the top of the hill, just a few hundred feet from her driveway, when they heard the familiar growl of a tractor coming down the road. Her heart skipped. Tilly had said Jake was coming to work the fields by her house. It was probably him right now.

"My daddy," Taryn called out as soon as the tractor topped the hill. She grinned up at Miriam. "Let's run, and we can catch him."

Still clutching her rocks, Taryn took off, her ponytail bobbing with each step. She was heading straight for the lumbering tractor.

Miriam's heart jumped, and she sprinted after the little girl, catching her by the shoulder. "Don't, Taryn. What if he can't see you? He'll run right over you."

Taryn frowned up at Miriam. "Not my daddy. He sees everything."

As the tractor came closer, Miriam realized from Jake's glower that Taryn was right.

JAKE SLAMMED the throttle lever back, hit the clutch, and braked. Why was Taryn with Miriam? And where was Tilly? He put the tractor in park, took in a deep breath, and climbed out of the cab.

"Daddy, Daddy, look at the rocks I found." Taryn ran up to him, waiting, as he had taught her, a safe distance away from the wheels of the huge tractor.

He walked closer, pointedly ignoring Miriam as he took a moment to squat down and look at the rocks in his daughter's dirty hands. "They are very nice," he said, turning one over in his hand, then handing it back to Taryn.

"And Miriam was going to make a water wheel, but she didn't have her knife." Taryn bestowed an innocent smile on him, clutching her rocks back to her chest. "I said you have one. Can we use it?"

"Sure you can," Jake said absently as he straightened, finally looking over at Miriam, who stood a distance away. A safe distance, he thought, reaching automatically into the front pocket of his jeans to pull out his pocketknife. He walked over and handed it to her. "Taryn said you needed this?"

Miriam took it, avoiding his gaze. "We were going to make water wheels just after Tilly met me on the road." Miriam looked down at the knife, then up at him. "Fred isn't feeling good, and Tilly had to take him into town. She asked me to watch Taryn for her."

Jake heard Miriam's words, his heart tightening. Fred, sick again? It must be serious if Tilly was taking the time to run him in, and Fred was letting her.

He closed his eyes briefly, sending up a quick prayer. *Please, Lord. Don't let it be serious.* He opened his eyes and caught Miriam looking at him with that same wistful expression he had seen before. He felt a sudden desire to touch her, to reassure her himself. He had to stop himself from pulling her into his arms.

"You still have this," she said quietly, holding up his pocketknife. She looked up at him again, the spring breeze lifting strands of her hair.

"Yeah. It was the first birthday present I had gotten in a few years." He shrugged, willing away the attraction he felt for her.

She smiled then, running her thumb over the worn red plastic. "I remember saving up to buy it for you."

Once again, Jake suppressed the urge to touch her hair, to curve his hand around her neck. To pull her close.

Reconnect to the young, innocent woman who had given him that pocketknife, so proud that she had bought it for him.

He took a step back, as if afraid he had already done so. "I better get back to work," he said abruptly.

"Oh, and Tilly asked if I could bring you supper if she didn't get back on time." She chanced another glance up at him, adding, "If you don't mind, that is."

Jake felt a nudge of sorrow at the uncertainty on her face.

It made her look vulnerable. Not an emotion he would have associated with her at any time in her life. Not as a young girl, not as a woman. "No, that's okay." He waited as time seemed to drift away. Once again, they were young and in love. Once again, she smiled up at him, her eyes shining.

But he remembered the pictures in Paula's book: a girl made up and expensively dressed. He could pretend all he wanted, but this Miriam was far removed from him. He called a quick goodbye to his daughter and climbed back in the tractor.

Then he put the tractor in gear and turned into the field. Dropping the seeder down, he adjusted the depth and half turned to look behind him.

Miriam and Taryn stood on the road, watching him.

His past and his present, side by side.

For a moment, he wondered what his life would have been like had he and Miriam stayed together. Would that little girl have been theirs? Would they have had more?

"Don't be ridiculous, Jake," he said, switching on the radio. "She's in another realm now." And her leaving meant this land he now worked would be sold.

His day chugged along, punctuated by hourly news and weather reports. The songs melded one into the other, country songs usually, or classical music when he bothered to change the station.

Jake worked his way up and down the quarter of land, each time on his return watching out for Miriam and his daughter. He caught sight of them once, walking down the road, heading out, he suspected, to make the water wheel Taryn had spoken of. The sun gave off a sharp spring brightness, creating a feeling of expectation and promise, and he wished he could be with Taryn and Miriam, playing with the spring runoff, doing ordinary family things.

He tried to concentrate on his work but found his eyes

straying to the two figures as they made their way down the road, looking for all the world like a mother and daughter.

The next time he came back to the road, Miriam and Taryn were gone, and he felt as if the day had lost a measure of that brightness and expectation.

The sun slipped inexorably across the sky. By 5:30, Jake once again began watching the road for Miriam. It was because he was hungry, he told himself. But when he thought of spending another mealtime with her, he felt a burst of pleasure.

"You're a strange man," he said aloud, turning the wheel of the tractor at the end of the field. "And a very stupid one." He got the tractor straightened around and lined up, checking to make sure the seeder's depth was still good. The roar of the tractor's engine was the only sound he heard as he worked his way down the field. He was up and over the rise when he saw a car parked on the road. His spirits lifted despite his previous self-castigation.

He could just make out Miriam's slim figure, her hand up, shading her eyes against the lowering sun, watching him, waiting for him. It felt good to know she was there.

He parked the tractor and walked over. "Where's Taryn?" he asked as he approached.

"Playing in the ditch. We ate already. I've got your supper in the car," she said, walking over to it and opening the door. "I hope it's still warm." She pulled out an insulated cooler.

Jake walked around the car, and when she straightened, he was there to take the cooler from her. Startled, she took a step back and almost lost her balance. Jake caught her by the shoulders, and her head came up. Once again, their eyes held. Awareness arced between them. Jake didn't let go of her shoulders, and she didn't let go of the handles.

Her eyes were the same deep brown that he remembered, fringed with silky lashes, tilted up at the corners exotically. She still had a tiny mole at one corner of her eye; her cheek still sported the barely discernible scar from the time she bumped it on his truck door. The same light freckles were sprinkled across her forehead, and her lips still held…still held… Jake couldn't keep his eyes off her mouth. The way she nervously wet her lips. The way they parted slightly as her breath quickened.

"Please, Jake," she said quietly.

Jake looked up into her eyes again, his fingers tightening, his thumbs caressing her arms through the thin material of her sweater. Then, with a deep breath, he dropped his hands. What was wrong with him? He was acting as if they were both still teenagers. Still in love.

"Sorry," he said, taking the cooler from her. There was a moment of awkwardness as their hands meshed; she tried to let go and he tried to take hold.

"Look at what Miriam made me," Taryn trilled, skipping up to his side.

Jake put down the cooler, thankful for the diversion. "Wow. A willow whistle."

Taryn nodded. "Listen." She put it in her mouth and blew lightly. It gave a definite *tweet*, and Taryn grinned her pleasure. "Miriam made it for me outta a piece o' wood from the bush. She just cut it and made it. She said when the bark dries, it won't work anymore. You try it now." Taryn handed it to him, and Jake dutifully blew on the willow whistle.

The spicy smell, the smooth texture of the bark, and the faint bitter taste all took him back to other springs.

Other springs with Miriam. She was the only one he knew who could make these. He had asked her to teach him once, but she had played coy, telling him that it was one of her few talents and that she needed to keep some secrets.

He had never learned how to make them. He had one he had kept, but as Taryn said, once they got older, they didn't work. He hadn't blown on one since then.

Miriam was setting up lawn chairs beside him, and he

handed the whistle back to Taryn, who gave it another *tweet* and ran off back to the ditch for more treasures. Jake shifted to face Miriam.

"You still remember how to make those."

Miriam nodded. "I didn't think I would, but once I started, it all came back. My dad taught me well."

Jake watched as she snapped open her chair and set it on the gravel. "You seldom talked about your father."

Miriam bent over the cooler again. "I think coming back here made me realize I have more good memories than I thought." She looked up at him and ventured a half smile.

Jake felt it again—the awareness, the realization they had known each other in a different time and place, as different people.

They shared a past, memories, and an intimacy that he had never felt with anyone else, even Paula.

And for the first time since Miriam had come, he wondered if she had ever cared for anyone else. Had ever been close to another man.

He realized in the next moment that he didn't want to know.

Jake bent his head to eat and slowly relaxed, letting his thoughts rest, settle, and separate from the awareness of the girl sitting beside him.

"I should tell you, Tilly phoned," Miriam said quietly.

Jake lowered his fork, almost afraid to hear what she had to say.

Miriam frowned lightly. "Fred is still running a high fever. If it doesn't go down, they're going to send him to Calgary for some more tests. He's a strong man, Jake," she said reassuringly. "I'm sure he'll be okay."

"I pray he will," Jake replied, toying with the rest of his casserole.

"Tilly also told me that Fred had a heart attack a while

ago." Miriam's comment broke the silence. "I'm sure you're quite concerned about him now."

"I get afraid when I think about his health. Anything could happen." He looked out over the field, his legs stretched out in front of him, his plate balanced on his lap.

"How old is Fred now?" Miriam asked.

"About sixty." Jake sighed lightly. "Which used to seem very old when I was younger."

"Parents aren't supposed to get old or sick."

Jake glanced sidelong at Miriam, who leaned forward on her chair, elbows on her knees, her chin resting on her hands. She was staring out over the field, but Jake suspected she was thinking of her own mother.

"I never did tell you…I'm sorry about your mother." Jake shifted to face her, resisting the urge to touch her, to comfort her.

"It's been difficult…" Miriam stopped, her lower lip pulled between her teeth.

Jake didn't know what else to say. He had never cared for Miriam's mother, but he knew that Edna had been a strong force in Miriam's life. Now Edna was dead, and what had happened to him was long ago.

There were questions he wanted to ask Miriam, things he wanted to know.

And what would that accomplish? he thought, turning away again. *Do you want to find out how quickly she forgot you? Do you really want to know?*

His ego was as fragile as the next man's. Better let it sit. Once she left and the farm was sold, he would probably never see her again.

He finished what he could of his meal and got up, setting the plates inside the cooler. "Thanks for supper."

MIRIAM CLOSED the lid of the cooler and turned, just as Jake moved to pick it up. Their hands brushed each other. The simplest of touches, but she felt it like a jolt of electricity.

She yanked her hands back just as he did the same.

Did he feel it too?

Once again shaking off her reaction, she stepped aside, looking away while she heard him set in the car. He came back, and she turned to politely thank him, only to find him staring down at her, his expression unreadable.

"Have a good evening, Miriam," he said quietly.

His deep voice touched a memory. The high school dance. He had driven her home and insisted on walking her to the door.

She protested, not sure if her mother was up.

Instead, he brushed his hand through her hair, smiled at her, and said exactly the same words.

And then he kissed her.

Now, once again, he towered over her, his eyes delving deep into hers, searching. She couldn't look away.

He shifted his weight, coming closer. For a heart-stopping moment, Miriam thought he might kiss her again, the way he did ten years ago.

Then he blinked, gave a light shake of his head, and stepped back, making way for her to pass. She felt an illogical twinge of disappointment, then walked past him to Taryn.

"I'll be home in about an hour," Jake said behind her. "If Tilly isn't there, do you mind waiting with Taryn?"

"No," she said without turning. "Of course not. I can't leave her alone."

A beat of silence, then, "Thanks so much. For everything."

She chanced a look over her shoulder but avoided his eyes. "You're welcome," she returned, just loud enough for him to hear.

"Bye, Daddy. I'll see you later," Taryn called out.

By the time they got in the car, Jake was back in the tractor. As they drove away, Taryn turned to watch her father as they drove away from each other.

"I love my dad."

Her words flicked over Miriam's soul as she thought of her own father. And for a heartbreaking moment, she missed him. Deeply.

Wondered what he would have thought of Jake.

Tilly wasn't at the farmhouse by the time they got there, so Miriam ran a bath for Taryn and helped her get ready for bed, listening to the child chatter about the cows, the baby calves, and how much she loved her willow whistle, but she really loved her daddy more.

A few minutes later, Taryn was kneeling on her bed, pulling a scrapbook from under her pillow. "This is my mommy's book," Taryn said, eagerly holding it out to Miriam. "You want to look? There are pictures of you in it."

Miriam hesitated, not sure she wanted to delve back into the past.

"Please look," Taryn begged, giving her a pleading smile.

Miriam gave in, nodded, and Taryn dropped the book onto her lap.

Miriam wasn't eager to see what Paula might have put in the book, yet it held a strange fascination as Taryn flipped through the worn pages. She caught glimpses of Paula when she was younger, old school programs. Other pictures of her interspersed with articles. Stickers decorated the pages, and a few comments were written in.

Why did Paula want to know what her once friend was up to? Why did she go to the bother of cutting out pictures of her husband's old girlfriend?

Obviously, she had bought the magazines to cut said pictures out of.

Miriam wasn't naive enough to think that Paula kept them because of some sentimental attachment. The last phone conversation they had was full of Paula's crowing over the victory she had achieved.

She had gotten Jake to take her to the prom.

"Here. This is my favorite," Taryn said with a note of triumph.

Miriam looked down at a picture of herself on the arm of a well-known actor. She was leaning against him, clad in a shimmering sheath she wore on loan from a struggling designer.

Opposite it and on the following pages were advertisements she had done. These were followed by more of her at a charity function escorted by a well-known fashion designer. Her dress was low-cut and revealing. Also on loan from that designer.

Another of her at a gala, with two men flanking her. Both movie stars. Both intoxicated at the time.

Miriam felt a moment of shame, thinking that Taryn, this sweet innocent child, had seen this part of her life. A part that Miriam wasn't proud of and had spent the last few years trying to live down.

"You had lots of boyfriends, too," Taryn piped up. "You still have lots of boyfriends?"

"Not boyfriends," corrected Miriam sardonically. She closed the book and placed it on the side of the bed. "You don't need to keep this, do you?" She hated to think that Taryn had been exposed to a part of life that no girl of five should know about.

Taryn looked up at her, her expression hurt. "It was my mommy's."

Miriam felt instantly contrite. "Of course. That makes it special, doesn't it?" Miriam gave her a gentle smile, determined to prove herself worthy of this young child. "But you know what? Those pictures of me aren't who I am anymore. And they aren't the kind of pictures a little girl like you should see. They are all pictures of big people doing silly things. Things you don't need to see."

"Are they a sin?" she asked, her eyes wide.

Miriam repressed the urge to laugh yet realized she had never considered her life in such a harsh glare before. Was it "sin"?

She wasn't sure that she was ready to categorize it so bleakly. It certainly was far removed from the life she had lived here in Waylen—that much, she was willing to concede.

"It isn't a sin to look at those pictures," she said, neatly side-stepping Taryn's question. "But maybe we could take these ones of me out. Then it can be just a book about your mommy."

Taryn considered this a moment. "But I like you. And I want a picture of you."

"You know what?" Miriam said. "I have other pictures of me. I could send you some of those." She had enough comp cards—surely, she could find a recent one that made her look like a normal person instead of the party-hardy girl she used to be, flashing a fake smile and overly made up.

"Okay." Taryn smiled and snuggled down into her bed. "Now you have to say my prayers with me." She closed her eyes, her hands folded on her chest, and began singing.

The young voice breathlessly singing the familiar words of "Jesus Tender Shepherd" touched a chord deep in Miriam's heart. If she closed her eyes, she could remember the smell of fresh laundry and her father sitting beside her on the bed, singing the song that asked Jesus to stay with her through the darkness, thanking Him for His care during the day.

Miriam swallowed a lump of emotion, suddenly unable to sing along.

Taryn finished on her own and peeked up at Miriam. "You have to help me."

"I forgot the words," Miriam fibbed, sniffing lightly. "Now say the rest of your prayers."

Taryn closed her eyes and launched into a list of "please be with," and named Fred, Tilly, Jake, a few friends from play school, and then, to Miriam's surprise, Taryn asked God to be with Miriam, asked Him to make her happy and not so sad.

Miriam bit her lip, struggling against an unexpected wave of sorrow. To be prayed for, to have someone concerned about her—when had that last happened in her life?

Stop being so maudlin, she told herself.

Ah, the strong voice of reason. Miriam surreptitiously wiped her eyes, took a steadying breath, and waited for Taryn to finish her petitions.

When the child was done, she grinned up at Miriam again. "Are you going to kiss me goodnight?" she asked.

Miriam hesitated, seeing the danger in this simple action. As Jake had said, Taryn too easily became attached to people. Despite Tilly, Fred, and Jake's unwavering love, Miriam could see Taryn was hungry for the affection of a mother.

Something she couldn't give the sweet girl.

This was her chance to let Taryn know her stay was temporary and to reinforce what Jake had asked of her. "You know what I'll do instead," she said, her heart aching at the poignancy of the moment. "I'll give you a kiss in your hand, and you can use it whenever you want. Okay?" Miriam didn't wait for an answer; she lifted Taryn's small hand and carefully placed a kiss in it. Then she curled Taryn's fingers around it. "There. Now you have a kiss from me that you can use when I'm gone."

"Where are you going?"

"I don't live here. I'm only staying for a few more days. Then I have to go back to New York."

"But couldn't you stay? I want you to stay. I want you and my daddy..."

"Miriam doesn't live here, Pip."

Jake's deep voice from the doorway made Miriam jump.

How much had he heard? She glanced up at him, unable to stop the way her heart jumped at his presence.

He stood, leaning his shoulder in the doorway, hands tucked in the pockets of his jeans, his shirtsleeves rolled up, his shirt open at the neck. The light from the hallway threw his face into silhouette. In that moment, Miriam could see so clearly the difference between the boy she had loved and the man who now stood before her. His shoulders were broader, his chest deeper. Even his relaxed stance showed her a level of confidence that only comes with age.

It also made him that much more appealing.

"She's only here for a little while, and then she's going back to her home." Jake pushed himself away from the doorway and walked over to the bed. Miriam jumped up and stepped aside. But the room wasn't very large, and they bumped into each other in the process. Jake caught Miriam by the shoulders, and their eyes met.

It was only a split second, barely measured in a heartbeat, but in that moment, her awareness of him compounded. She almost stumbled but regained her balance, thankful for the subdued light in the bedroom. No one could see Miriam Spencer, one-time It Girl and cover model, blushing at the touch of a man who still smelled like the dirt he had been seeding in all day. A man whose chin was rough with stubble, whose eyes seemed to burn into her.

A man who didn't want her around.

Miriam's heart stuttered at the thought, then she said a quick goodnight to Taryn and left. Once downstairs, she couldn't decide whether she should leave right away or stay. Politeness deemed that she at least say goodnight to Jake, but she didn't know if she wanted to face him.

She cleaned up the kitchen, glad to keep busy, and, before she was finished, Jake came down the stairs.

"She settled in now?"

Jake nodded and dropped wearily onto a chair, tunneling

his hands through his hair. He looked tired. She was sure he was thinking of Fred.

Miriam felt a surge of protectiveness toward him, a desire to run her hands over his head, to tidy the unruly waves, to tell him that everything would be okay.

He looked up at her, his mouth curved into a wry smile. "I want to thank you for taking care of Taryn. I've had a lot on my mind."

Miriam clutched the towel closer, then gave into her impulse and walked over to the table, sat beside him, and covered his hand with hers. She was simply comforting him, she told herself.

"Fred is strong, Jake. I'm sure he'll be fine."

Jake squeezed her hand gently, and she was about to pull away when he turned her palm over, running his thumb over her hand.

"I want to thank you for your help. I know I asked you to stay away from Taryn, but..." His voice trailed off.

She didn't want to feel a thrill at the warm touch of his hands, didn't want to look up into his eyes and feel lost again. But she did.

And as their eyes melded, time swirled around her, past blending with present. Old emotions bringing out new.

But over all this, she keenly felt the reality of her situation. The business debt that always hovered and how it came about.

It was wise to remember that. Jake was a good father, and she knew that she wasn't the kind of person he would marry. Not anymore.

The thought cut her deep into her soul, searing and painful. She didn't want to feel unworthy. She had spent enough of her youth carrying that stigma. Her mother unwittingly reinforced every teasing comment from schoolmates by criticizing her clumsiness, her inability to meet her mother's exacting standards. Miriam had managed to ignore her fellow students and to laugh off their comments, but her mother's had buried deep into her psyche.

Until Jake.

He had been the first man she had ever loved. The first person who had considered her beautiful, caring, and worthy.

Jake continued to play with her hand, his touch sending shivers curling through her. "I don't imagine you've had much chance to be around kids, yet you certainly have a way with Taryn." He smiled carefully and tilted his head to one side, as if studying her. "What you did upstairs with her was a lesson in diplomacy and tact."

Miriam shrugged the comment away, even as it warmed her to the very fingertips Jake now held. Praise from Jake always did that to her. Silly that even now, it could move her more than any compliment from a photographer or her agent. "She's a sweet child and very intelligent. I do find I have to be careful with her."

"And you have been." He held her eyes with his, his mouth quirking up in a half smile. "Thanks again."

Miriam couldn't have looked away if she'd tried. She wanted to say something to lighten the atmosphere, to give herself some emotional edge.

Instead, she leaned forward, giving in to the attraction that was building within her, hoping she could pull this off. Be casual about it.

"Thanks, yourself," she said quietly, pressing a light kiss to his forehead. But then she inhaled the earthy, farmer smell of him, her confidence wavering, her senses heightened by the contact.

Jake snaked a hand around her neck, capturing her. "Why did you do that?" His velvet brown eyes delved into hers.

Miriam allowed herself a small dream, a tiny reaching toward the unattainable, and stroked his thick hair away from his face, the way she always used to do. "For old times' sake," she whispered, her voice catching.

Jake's eyes darkened as tension built.

"If we're really going back to old times' sake…" He let the sentence trail off as he slowly, gently pulled her head down and touched his lips to hers, his breath warm on her mouth.

His warm, soft lips moved over hers, entreating, compelling. Miriam's hands went slack, then she reached up, threading her fingers through his thick hair, anchoring his head as her own mouth returned his caress.

The kiss gained urgency, their lips hungry now, moving, demanding.

What are you doing?

Reality cut through the cocoon of ardor they had spun.

But Miriam didn't want to acknowledge it, didn't want to pull away. Jake's hand on her neck, his mouth on hers—these were so achingly familiar and so dear. His touch answered a longing that no one else had or ever would.

But the little girl sleeping in this house, his obligations, all slid into the moment. He wasn't for her, and she wasn't staying.

She dropped her hand and lowered her head, breaking the contact.

His hand clenched into a fist on his knee, and she wanted to touch it, to smooth away the tension she saw there. But she had caused it, she was sure, and would not be able to offer any respite.

"Why, really, did you come back, Miriam?" he asked, his voice hoarse with repressed emotion.

Miriam's heart skipped as she wondered what she dared tell him and still keep her dignity and her heart intact.

"Did you come here just to sell the farm?" Jake looked up at her. "You could have done that from out east. You say you came for a break, but I sense there's more going on. Was it a man that caused this unspoken pain I sense in you?"

Miriam closed her eyes at how close he had struck with his comment, yet how far off he was. If she said "yes," he would assume she was acknowledging a broken heart, and he would let go of her hand. Leave her alone.

But this kitchen, his rough hand holding hers, brought back a flood of bittersweet memories. Memories of stolen kisses and whispered promises. Memories of a love that still haunted her.

And though what she had to say would make her vulnerable to him, she knew she had to finish this right now if she was to go back with any measure of peace.

She had to ask the questions that haunted her still.

"I guess I wanted to find out about you and Paula," she said quietly. "I had a foolish hope of reconciling with her and you. But I can't talk to her, so there's only you. I want to find out why you broke up with me. Why you married her."

Jake's head shot up, and his hands tightened on hers.

As their eyes met, Miriam wondered if she had done the right thing.

Chapter 8

$\mathcal{J}$ake held her gaze, trying to marshal his thoughts. Sort through how to tell her and what to tell her.

"Why didn't you write me?" he countered.

"Are you kidding?" Miriam stood and shoved the chair back, and Jake saw a brief flash of the old Miriam. "You break up with me, and you expect *me* to write *you?* Why weren't you upfront with me? Tell me that Paula was the one you loved."

"She wasn't," was all he could manage.

Miriam's eyes narrowed, then she released a harsh laugh.

"I was such a silly girl. You promised you would love me forever. Why did I believe you? When you ended our relationship, why didn't you care enough to be honest, to—?" Her voice broke on that last word, and her hands flew to her face, covering her shame, her pain.

Jake felt his own heart twist at the sound of her voice, the sight of her anger and anguish. He was surprised at the strength of her emotions. Why should it matter after all this time?

He was unsure what to do. She leaned against the kitchen

counter, the muted sounds of her cries fastening on his soul like barbed hooks.

He got up, walked toward her, and carefully, gently, took her in his arms. At first, she resisted, her shoulders hunched, her hands still clutched over her face.

"I'm sorry you saw it that way. So sorry." He continued to hold her, to stroke her back, and slowly, imperceptibly, the tension holding her in its thrall loosened, and finally she curled against him and lay her head against his shoulder. Her slender arms slipped around him, and Jake let his eyes drift shut as she clung to him, his own arms tightening, holding her as close as he dared.

"What a mess this all turned out to be," he muttered.

She drew in a shuddering breath, then another. She pulled away, swiping at her face, her hair tousled, her mascara a black smudge, her eyes red.

And yet, she never looked more appealing.

She lifted her chin, eyes holding his, hands clenched at her side, eyes hard now.

"If you are telling me the truth, that you didn't love Paula, why did you date her so soon after I left? Why did you marry her?"

Jake didn't want to talk about Paula. Didn't want to bring her between them again. If Miriam was leaving, what did it matter?

But he couldn't bear to see the disdain in her eyes one second longer. For her to believe this lie.

"I…had my reasons."

"Well, let's vague it up," she interrupted. Then she shook her head, huffing out an annoyed breath. "Okay. Let's back up then. Tell me why you broke up with me."

Again, he felt he had to sift through his memories. Try to find the right way to say what she was looking for. Words weren't his strong suit, but he had to do his best.

"You need to know I didn't want to. I felt pushed into a corner."

"By who? Me?"

"You were the one who wanted to run away," he returned. "And I wasn't about to leave the only home I ever knew." Too late, he realized how defensive he sounded, then raised his hands, as if to smooth away his awkward words.

"And that's the only reason you broke up with me?" She frowned at him. "I wish you would have told me. It would have made a difference."

Jake couldn't stop the flicker of hope her words gave him, but extinguishing that faint glimmer came reality.

"It might have," was all he could offer.

Miriam frowned at his vague comment. "Why do I feel like there's something you're not telling me?"

He waited another beat, then shook his head, not sure what to say or how.

But Miriam wouldn't let him off the hook. Her eyes bored into his. "What else happened?"

He paused, holding her intense gaze, then realized he had nothing to lose. Her mother was gone, and he knew that she and Miriam had a complicated relationship.

But he also knew he had to tread carefully.

"I don't know how else to say this, but your mother was part of the reason I broke up with you as well." Probably the biggest reason but to admit the hold she'd had over him was, in retrospect, embarrassing.

"How was she possibly to blame?"

Another hesitation and with a shrug, he let the words come out in a rush, before he changed his mind again. "She met me after school one day and said we needed to talk. I followed her as she walked along the sidewalk. Then when we were far enough away from the school that you probably couldn't see us, she told me to stay away from you. Said she had found out about our relationship and told me to stop seeing you. She told me that she had all these big plans for you and that I was getting in the way."

The fight seemed to sift out of Miriam at that. "What did you tell her?"

Jake looked past her, going back to that humiliating but heart-searing conversation. "I knew what I was, what I didn't have," he continued, not answering her question. Needing to explain. "I was turning eighteen in the summer. When that happened, Fred and Tilly would no longer be responsible for me. I would be on my own. What could I offer you? When you came up with that half-baked scheme about running away —I have to confess, for a moment, I thought of it, too." He released a harsh laugh and pushed on. "I also knew that running away never solved anything. It only got Simon in trouble. I knew I had to wait and see what was going to happen in my life. Things were uncertain. I couldn't count on Fred and Tilly. That wasn't fair. And your mother…" He stopped. Her mother was dead. He had told her enough. Anything more felt like ·piling on was and didn't solve anything.

"What about her?"

"Doesn't matter," Jake said quietly.

"Yes it does, Jake."

To his shock, a tear slid down her cheek even as her eyes held his. She ignored it and pulled in a shaky breath. He wanted nothing more than to pull her into his arms and comfort her, but he also knew he had to wait. See where things went. He felt as if they were both edging toward a truth that could change so much for them.

"I know she had a lot to do with how my life ended up," Miriam continued, her gaze intent. "When she was dying, I tried to ask her, but she couldn't tell me. You have to. I need this finished. The book closed."

Jake drew in a deep breath and despite her encouragement, turned away from Miriam, his mind going back to that evening when he found out what Edna Spencer really thought of him.

"She told me that I didn't deserve you, and at the time, I thought she was right."

"She was wrong," Miriam interjected. "She had no right."

Jake had to smile at her defense, but he knew he had to finish this.

"Thanks for that, but there's more. And this was the biggest problem for me. She warned me that if I continued seeing you, she would cause problems for me with social services. Tell them that I was…well…taking advantage of you."

Miriam's gasp reinforced the concern and fear he felt at the time.

He plowed on. "I was scared. I was afraid she would get me kicked out of Fred and Tilly's place, and I had no other place to go. I didn't want to talk to Fred and Tilly about it because I didn't trust them. But I also knew your mom was right. What she had planned for you was bigger than anything I could ever offer."

He shrugged, rubbing the back of his neck. "I thought the best thing for both of us was for me to let go of you and give you a chance at something else." He pulled his hand over his face and blew out his breath. "I thought that maybe someday, I could make something of myself and come and get you. Letting you go was one of the hardest things I ever had to do. Then you left, and I never heard anything more." He turned to face her, his eyes holding hers, his own questions hovering. "Was you becoming a model part of your mother's plan for you? Because, to be honest, it was one of the last things I ever figured you would do."

Miriam leaned against the counter, looking away from him, her arms wrapped around her midsection. He also caught a glimmer of anger on her features.

"There were a hundred things going on. I was living with

my aunt and uncle, far away from you. You had broken up with me. I was mixed up and confused. I was doing poorly in school and wasn't sure where I would end up either." She angled him a wry smile. "You weren't the only one insecure about their future." She looked away again, twirling a strand of hair around her finger, a gesture he recognized from when she was upset and not sure what to say. But he let her carry on. "I heard about you and Paula and knew I wasn't coming back. Then Mom joined me. I moved in with her, and she got sick. Things were tough. When I got scouted by a modelling agency, I saw this as my chance to help us out. To maybe get her set up." She stopped there, her voice wavering, and Jake resisted the urge to touch her. Comfort her. He had his own ghosts to deal with before he could do that.

"I know I don't have any right to know, but why did you marry her?" Miriam continued.

The sorrow in her voice echoed the pain in his heart.

He didn't know precisely how he was going to explain. "After you left, Paula made no secret of how she felt about me. That she liked me. She was…well…relentless."

He turned to face her. But Miriam was now pressed back against the counter, her arms wrapped around her waist. Definitely defensive.

"I knew she liked you, but what are you trying to tell me?"

Jake couldn't hold back and reached out to touch her, to rebuild some connection, and Miriam flinched away. He had hoped that what he had said would ease some of the tension, but instead it increased it. So, he kept going. "I'm not proud of those few moments in my life," he said, his mind ticking back to those horrible, empty months. "I was missing you. You hadn't written. I didn't know where you were. I'm guessing your cell phone number changed because I couldn't even text you. I was lonely, and I didn't know what to do anymore. After you left, everything changed. Fred and Tilly had told me they were sending me to agricultural college and that they wanted me to stay with them after that. They wanted to tell me at prom. As a graduation gift. Fred wanted me to run the farm with him." He laughed, a bitter sound. "If he had told me that a month sooner, things would have been so different for us." He carefully pulled her hand away from her waist, taking it in his own, needing to make a connection with her while he spoke. "If I had known I had a future here, that I had security, I would have stood up to your mother."

"Why didn't you, anyway?"

"I was a foster child, and I had lived in enough foster homes to learn to keep things to myself. You don't ask about the future because no one can tell you. You have no legal rights, and your foster parents have no legal responsibilities. I had lived with Fred and Tilly for four years, yet I still hadn't learned to fully trust them." Jake stroked her fingers with his, his eyes on her hands.

"And where does Paula fit into all of this?"

He had to tell her everything.

"Yes, Paula." He laughed shortly. "She asked me to the prom, and I said yes. I was lonely, and I missed you. Shortly after that, we ended up at a party together. I thought you were living it up in the east, happy without me. I thought this was the glorious future your mom had planned." He rubbed his neck, sighing. "At this party, I started drinking, and the next thing I knew, I woke up in my truck. She was with me."

Miriam pulled her hand out of his, a soft cry escaping her lips.

"I know now that nothing happened," Jake said quickly, wanting to get past that part of the story and how it might look to her. "But at the time, she had me convinced that we had been intimate. That she might be pregnant. I felt I had to do the honorable thing and offer to marry her. I was young, scared, and thinking I would lose my chance with Fred and Tilly. I didn't realize then that I wouldn't have, and that I'd always underestimated the power of their love for me.

Always." He pulled in a deep breath. "Turned out Paula wasn't pregnant, and I felt betrayed. Trapped. But I was going to make this work. However, Paula and I didn't have a great marriage. It was okay at first, and when Taryn came, I thought things would change, but what she had done always hung between us. I tried, but I know I didn't try hard enough. She said she felt tied down by the farm. By Taryn. So, she would leave for a couple of weeks for a break. When she came back, and she always did, I was determined to try again. And again, things would be okay for a couple of weeks, then she'd get antsy, and pretty soon, she'd be gone. The last time she left, I begged her to stop doing this. She got angry and stormed out the door. Two hours later, the police were at the door, and Paula was in the hospital. Gone."

"Oh, Jake. I'm so sorry."

For a moment, he relived the confusion of emotions from that time. Sorrow, regret, all tinged with a guilty relief.

"In spite of all of that, I have Taryn," he continued. "I will always thank the Lord for her. The beauty that came out of the ashes."

Silence again. Miriam sighed lightly, her hand rubbing her forehead, back and forth, back and forth.

"What a mess," she said softly.

Jake silently agreed.

They stood in silence, Jake trying to mentally meld what he knew about Miriam's life with what he had once believed; he prayed she was doing the same.

And what was going to come of this heart-to-heart? Love might conquer all in songs, but for him and Miriam, it seemed, there was too much history to get past. He had wanted to clear the air between them, to lay old ghosts to rest. She had come to do the same.

But now, after talking with her, he wondered if they would ever have a chance.

Miriam pushed herself away from the counter and

stopped a moment in front of Jake. She laid her hand on his shoulder and looked up at him.

Jake knew he should let her go, but he couldn't. He looked at Miriam, letting his eyes linger on her face, the features that were so much hers and yet older, harder.

He reached out to touch her, just once. That was all he meant to do. Then, as his hand lightly cupped her cheek, she caught his wrist, holding his hand against her. She sighed lightly, turning her head just enough to kiss the palm of his hand.

Her gesture pulled him toward her. And once again, he curled his hand around her neck. Once again, he dared to pull her head nearer. She didn't resist, and it was his undoing. Their breaths mingled for only a moment, then he carefully touched his mouth to hers, the familiarity of it rocking him.

Then he slipped his arms around her, pulling her closer, holding her tighter as his mouth moved against hers. She clung to him, returning his kiss, her fingers threading through his hair, capturing his head.

It wasn't enough—it was just a teasing hint of what they had missed all those years apart. Jake kissed her again and again, his mouth moving over hers. Then he pulled away, ignoring Miriam's muted cry of protest, kissing her cheek, her forehead, her eyes, curving her head into his neck and holding her tightly against him.

"Oh, Miriam," he said. "I wanted to do this the first time I saw you on the road."

She said nothing, only clung to him, her movements almost desperate.

Then, suddenly, she pulled away, taking his arms and drawing them away from her. She touched his mouth with her fingers, as if to capture the kiss he gave her, slowly traced the line of his lips, then, without saying another word, turned and walked out of the house.

Jake felt bereft as he watched her get in her car and drive

away, dirt spinning, gravel flying out behind her. She fish-tailed at the end of the driveway, then turned and drove away.

Jake took a long, slow breath. *I don't know what just happened, Lord, but be with her,* he prayed quietly. *Hold her in Your hands. Take care of her.* He drew in a deep breath. *Help me, as well.* He didn't know what he needed, but he knew that he had to swallow his own pride and go one step farther.

He had to talk with Miriam about the future—and that thought frightened him more than anything.

MIRIAM STEPPED on the accelerator as her car hurtled along. She drove without a destination, outrunning what lay behind her.

She felt as if her breath were still trapped in her chest, a heavy disquiet stirring deep within her. What she and Jake had shared in the past hour had completely switched and realigned her world.

All her perceptions, her ideas, had rearranged, and she had discovered one irrefutable fact.

She loved Jake Steele.

She slowed, wavering, her hand clenched to her heart. Oh, how she still loved him.

A deer, startled by her headlights, bolted in front of her. Miriam braked and swerved, narrowly missing it. She slammed on the brakes and rocked to a halt, dropping her head on the steering wheel.

She drew in a long, shuddering breath and slowly sat up. The quiet hum of the car and the glow of the dashboard lights created a safe place.

Just as it had been a haven to her as she drove to Waylen, this car was her escape now.

Miriam turned off the engine and the lights of her car.

The moon was waning, a thin sliver of light in a sky scattered with crushed stars.

She stepped out and let her eyes adjust to the heavy darkness. The silence pressed in on her, broken only by the faint croaking of frogs in a marsh below her.

She was close to Rock Lake, she realized, slowly able to make out a few more landmarks. She crossed the road and scrambled through the ditch, still soggy from spring runoff. A fence blocked her way, but she climbed over it, disregarding the barbs on the wire.

Miriam walked slowly along the field, staying close to the edges, her eyes on the ground. By the time she got to the top of the hill, her eyes had adjusted. The cool evening breeze was stronger here on the top of the hill, and she shivered, pulling her coat closer.

Below her, yard lights winked, scattered across the landscape, each representing a farmer's yard. There were more than when she used to come up here as a much younger girl.

Miriam pulled her coat down and slowly sat, pulling her knees close to her, dropping her head back.

Above her hung infinite stars like crushed diamonds flung across velvet, layer upon layer going far beyond what her fragile and mortal eye could see. Her mind knew what each of those tiny pinpoints of light represented, their size, their distance a number she couldn't get her mind around. And this was only a small part of our galaxy. There were as many galaxies as there were stars. She closed her eyes a moment, growing dizzy as she tried to fathom the depth of the skies around her.

Opening her eyes again, she easily found the Big Dipper wheeling slowly around the North Star; from there, the Little Dipper's Ursa Minor, then to Vega, Deneb, the constellation Cassiopeia. Her favorite, Orion the hunter, was a winter constellation and no longer visible.

She remembered lying out on sleeping bags outside with a

flashlight and a star book her father had bought her. When she was older, she used to impress Jake with her knowledge of the night sky. She used to wish she could be an astronaut and fly, fly away from here, away from her mother's petty restrictions, constant criticism, and harping.

Miriam bit her lip, guilt stopping her memories. Her mother was dead. In the weeks before she died, Edna had tried to apologize, had tried to explain why she pushed Miriam so hard. Miriam still didn't understand, and seeing Jake—the man her mother had so feared and disliked, the man she had once loved, the man whose life her mother had threatened to destroy—made Miriam feel as if, once again, she had to forgive her mother.

Seventy-times-seven.

The formula came back from old readings of the Bible. "I've done this already," she said aloud, looking up at the sky as if speaking to God. "I've forgiven her again and again. Will it never be over? Will I never be finished with this anger, this feeling of unfinished business?"

She stopped, as if waiting for an answer, her hands two tight balls of tension, her teeth pressed against each other. "I hated her so long—she took so much away," Miriam said again, her voice quieter.

The silent stars wheeled slowly on, unconcerned, timeless, vast.

She was just a small speck in this cosmos, unimportant, unnecessary. She had made sacrifices for her mother and in the process had lost the one thing she wanted.

Jake's love.

She loosened her fingers and caught her knees, resting her chin on them as she studied the vaguely lit land below.

Closing her eyes, she resurrected the touch of Jake's lips on hers, his hand on her neck. A thrill shivered through her at the memory. It had been so easy, so familiar.

There had been no awkwardness. No hesitation. No words

spoken, no promises made. Just a memory for her to hold onto…for the next ten years. The emptiness of the life that lay ahead of her became suddenly unbearable.

"What am I going to do?" she cried out. "Oh, Lord, You've got to help me."

Her cry had become a prayer, and she repeated it. "Please help me. I have fought being unworthy all my life. I've struggled with feeling unwanted, feeling ugly, feeling like a failure, feeling alone. I can't do that again."

Each time she saw Jake pray, each time she saw him with his daughter and saw the absolute love he showed her, each time she saw his devotion to Tilly and Fred, it was a reminder of who he was. A man with a sincere faith, a devotion to family.

And here she was—a woman who lived a life of selfishness, of vanity. After her mother's stroke, Miriam had visited her only rarely, using her busy schedule as an excuse. Then even those few visits had become more sporadic. She had wasted money, time, and much of her earlier years thinking only of herself. Self-preservation, she had called it, and it was necessary in the cutthroat world of high fashion.

Or so she had told herself.

Her clothing business was to be her escape from that world, a chance to slow down and enjoy life, to be her own person.

But now, it was as if the weight of the world lay on her narrow shoulders, each bill an immense boulder pressing down. Ten years of hard work had gotten her a car—fully paid for—a year's lease on an apartment in New York—paid for, albeit for now—but every piece of clothing she owned, every luxury, had come at a cost. Now thousands of dollars in bills soaked up any extra money she made. Bills for which she was personally responsible. The business she thought would give her freedom now felt like chains she could not escape from.

It was then that she had met Carl. Or actually, he had met her. He had found her and had convinced her to let him become her new agent. Miriam had resisted going back to modeling, going back to becoming a thing, an object—but Carl was different. Carl had spoken of a God who cared. A God who saw her as valuable and wonderful, just as she was.

Miriam had spoken to some of his other clients, had run a check on him and found out that he was not only legitimate but well-liked and respected in the fashion industry.

So, she signed on with him. He got her some well-paying jobs. She took everything that came her way, working herself to exhaustion at times. A few bills got paid, but the financial mountain seemed endless. Impossible.

Even worse, she couldn't shake the emptiness that haunted her.

One evening, as she sat in Carl's office, fighting tears of weariness and loneliness, he had told her to go home. To catch her breath, to sell her farm, and then, when all that was done, to come back. Pay down the loans. Get the monkey off her back.

As well, he had a line on an upcoming big job that would help her get through this financial crisis she was in right now.

She hesitated. She could have sold the farm from there, but she also knew she needed a break from the relentless grind of work and fear.

And while going back meant seeing Jake, a corner of her heart wanted to. Wanted to show herself that he didn't have that hold on her he used to.

But now, after being here a few days, she felt worse off than before.

Falling in love with Jake was all wrong. She was in no position to make herself vulnerable to him again. She was in no position to give him anything. Once he had said he had nothing to give her. Now it was she who not only had nothing to give but came with debt, money problems, and a lifestyle she couldn't seem to shake. She was all wrong for him.

What she had discovered tonight had completely changed the way she thought of him: he hadn't married Paula out of love but because he'd been coerced.

Miriam clenched her fists in anger, pressing them against her forehead at the thought of her friend's duplicity, her mother's scheming and pressure. How could she and Jake ever hope to get past this? It seemed too big a barrier. How could God have allowed all this to happen?

She looked up, past the stars to where she figured God was, removed from the miseries of common people like her and Jake. *Please help me, Lord. I know I haven't talked to You a lot, but I don't know where else to turn.* She hadn't prayed for so long; she knew this wasn't precisely the way, but she didn't know how else to go about it. *Please help me. I don't know what to think. I don't know what to do.*

She reached out with her mind, stretching, pulling, striving, wondering if God heard or if He cared.

Chapter 9

"$\mathcal{I}$ sure appreciate your taking time out to help me," Dane said to Jake. "For a while, I thought I might have to feed the calves for another week or so until I found someone who could move them to pasture for me."

Jake glanced at his neighbor and shrugged. "No problem, Dane. Glad to help." He had to say it. It was a problem. He was not yet done seeding. Rain was in the forecast, and he really wanted to get the seed in the ground before that came. Normally, he would have said no to Dane, but his tractor broke down yesterday, and he was waiting for a part that wasn't available for a few days.

So, he'd agreed to help Fred's old friend and try not to get fussed about the work hanging over him.

Dane Rogers was an older man who lived alone and had done so all his life. He was pushing eighty-five, yet he still farmed his own land, raised some calves, and in general enjoyed his life.

"I heard Fred wasn't doing so good. How is he now?" Dane asked as they stood enjoying the sun and the slight breeze that kept the bugs away.

Jake shook his head, watching the few stragglers pair up.

"They kept him in the hospital overnight a few days back, just to keep an eye on him. They were talking about doing tests, but he came home yesterday. He says he's okay. We'll see what happens."

"Life sure keeps a man busy, don't it?" Dane said. "I heard Miriam Spencer is back at her mom's place."

Jake gave the older man a sidelong glance. "You hear a lot for someone who doesn't get out much."

Dane grinned, hooking his thumbs in his ever-present suspenders. "Got me a cell phone. I stay in touch."

"I'm sure you do. Anything else you heard that you figure I need to know?"

"Well, I'm sure you know Miriam is still single." Dane elbowed him lightly, and Jake sighed. "She used to like you, didn't she? Surprises me that a girl that good-looking hasn't matched up with anyone. Makes you wonder, don't it?"

It hadn't made Jake wonder. Not until Dane mentioned it. He had assumed that Miriam had had boyfriends, that she had dated, but he had never wanted to speculate on why she was still single. He knew what Dane was hinting at, but since Miriam had come home, he hadn't dared let his speculation run that far.

"She's only here for a while. She's selling her farm and heading back east to make more money." Jake couldn't keep the harshness from his voice. The other night, and the nights since, he had lain in bed, reliving every moment with Miriam, what they had talked about, unable to come to a solution.

It seemed that too much hung between them, that the barriers were insurmountable. Yet he couldn't help but remember her response to him.

Her tears. The kiss they shared that still felt like it lingered on his lips.

And the fact that she was still single, as Dane so thoughtfully pointed out. He had kept himself busy, had tried not to look too interested when Tilly talked of Miriam's visits.

"Oh, I'm sure you could talk her out of leaving. You're still a good-looking young man." Dane clapped a companionable hand on Jake's shoulder. "Give it a whirl. What have you got to lose?"

My pride, Jake thought. Yet even as that idea formed, he knew it was a small price to pay. Thinking about Miriam leaving gave him a hollow feeling that grew each day, each hour.

Jake shrugged, as if to dispel the sensation. "I've got enough on my mind right now, Dane. I don't know if I have the will or energy to go courting."

"She lives just down the road. How much work could it be?" Dane chuckled. "Tell Tilly to have her over for supper. Take her for a ride in your tractor."

"And isn't that romantic," said Jake wryly, walking over to his truck.

"What I remember of you two, it used to be."

Jake smiled, remembering, too. "Right about now, I've got to fix my tractor, get my crop in, check my own cows, and try to figure out how I'm going to replace the land she's selling. Seems like enough to keep me busy." He got into the truck and rolled down the window. "You let me know if you need anything else, okay?"

Dane leaned his arms on the window frame, shaking his head. "No time to court a pretty girl but figures he has time to offer to help me. You got your priorities all mixed up, my boy."

Jake laughed lightly. "I've got to go, Dane. I'll follow you out and then shut the gate for you."

"I can do that myself, you young punk."

"Okay." Jake put the truck in gear and slowly pulled away. He swung the truck and the long fifth-wheel trailer around, then headed out the gate and down the road. He glanced in his side mirror and saw Dane pull out behind him and shut the gate.

Satisfied, he sped up. He had hoped to check his own cows this afternoon and then run back into town for a part for his tractor. Maybe tomorrow he could get the Spencer field done. Then it would be Sunday again.

And shortly after that, Miriam was leaving.

He clutched the steering wheel, forcing himself to stay focused. They each had their own lives, he reminded himself. They each had their own responsibilities. She had been back barely a week. He must be crazy to think that just because mistakes of the past had been talked about, all was cleared away. Miriam had run away that night and stayed away. That told him, more clearly than anything she could have said, what she wanted.

She didn't fit, didn't belong.

Yet even as he thought that, he remembered how good she was with Taryn, how easily she seemed to fit in to the farm life. He remembered her feeding his cows. He still had to smile at the sight of her in her expensive clothes, manhandling that tractor around the yard; she was as small as ever and still had to stand up to steer.

He had felt guilty that day. Felt as if he had ditched his responsibilities and she'd had to cover for him.

Yet it made him feel like the two of them, for a brief moment, had shared this part of his life. He felt like what he did was important to her.

Get a grip, Steele. You really are delusional, he thought, gearing down as his truck powered out on the hill.

THE SUN BEAT down on Jake's head as he clucked to Pinto. The horse flicked its ears, looked back, and then started walking down the trail to the road. He slowed the horse down, reluctant to be drawn back into the rush and pressure that exemplified planting season. Fred had often told him that somehow it always got done. Seed time and harvest, the ebb and flow of the cycle, always happened. And the few times it didn't, it was often because of measures beyond their control. He was waiting to hear from the tractor dealership. They had a shipment coming in later today. His part might be with it.

Fred was feeling much better, and he and Tilly had taken Taryn to a birthday party at a friend of Tilly's. Jake had offered, but Taryn didn't seem too eager to have him come along.

Which meant Jake was at loose ends.

Which meant he could go out. Maybe check the Spencer fields, which, if he were honest, was just an excuse to hopefully see Miriam.

So, he'd saddled Pinto and headed out, struggling to tamp down the anticipation that was growing. Trying not to assume anything.

Trying not to think too much about the kisses they shared, the confidences that had eased away so much of the unanswered questions that had plagued him for the last many years. Nothing definitive had come out of it and yet, so much had changed.

Jake drew a deep breath and sent up a prayer of thanksgiving for this beautiful day and for possibilities. For the first time in years, he felt hope was lingering, teasing him. The road was quiet, and Pinto seemed content to simply plod along. The birds seemed especially chipper, and their tweets and calls followed him as the sun warmed his back.

He pulled his horse to a stop at a rise, his hands resting on the pommel of the saddle, Dane's words ringing through his head. He was unable to dispel the memory of Miriam in his arms.

Courtship. He and Miriam had missed out on that when they started going out. They had had to keep their relationship a secret and thus had never indulged in the fun stuff that came with dating.

Did he dare open himself up to her like that?

What would he gain and what would he lose?

Pinto shook her head, her bridle jangling, and snorted as Jake sifted through the reasons for and against.

It would be so much easier just to keep on going. But to what end? He loved Taryn. He loved Fred and Tilly.

But he also knew that deep inside, he yearned for someone who would be his partner in many senses of that word. Someone who would miss him and whom he would look forward to seeing at the end of the day. Someone who would sit with him on the couch and talk to him about her day. Listen to him talk about his.

All those roles were filled in one way or another by his daughter and his parents. Yet Tilly had Fred, and Taryn was slowly growing up and away from him. That was nature.

He was all alone in a family.

Yet, if he were to give in to his growing feelings for Miriam, and she left anyway, how would he manage? He had been desolated when she left the first time. He was older and less flexible now. It would be harder this time.

Because whether he liked to admit it or not, he was falling in love with her again. And he knew this time around it was different. Deeper and stronger.

He closed his eyes, letting the memories of the other night drift around him, hold him, as Miriam's arms had held him. He knew that she cared. Something held her back, and the only way he would find out what was to spend time with her.

Starting now, he thought, pulling Pinto's head around.

The horse trotted down the driveway. When they got to the maple tree, he stopped.

Miriam sat underneath it, a book open on her lap, her eyes shut.

Jake wondered if she was sleeping, but then he saw her lift her head. "Hey, there," he said quietly, hoping he wouldn't startle her.

Miriam looked up, her hand on her chest, her mouth and eyes wide open.

He did scare her.

"Oh, my goodness. You scared the living daylights out of me," she said weakly.

Jake dismounted and tied Pinto to a nearby tree, then walked across the lawn to her. Miriam stayed where she was, her hand still on her chest.

"I didn't even hear you coming," she said, avoiding his gaze.

"I thought at first you were sleeping."

"No. Just sitting and thinking." She moved to get up, but Jake stopped her with a hand on her shoulder. He sat down beside her, his legs crossed. He pointed to the book on her lap. "A little light reading?"

"It's my mom and dad's Bible. Hardly light," Miriam replied, her fingers fiddling with the pages. "Found it in a box I was going through."

"So, what have you…" He hesitated, cleared his throat, and tried again. "What have you been reading?"

"Just skipping through. Catching stuff here and there."

"What are you looking for?"

Miriam shook her head as she flicked through the pages. "I don't know," she whispered. "Comfort. Absolution."

"What do you mean?"

Miriam shook her head. "Nothing. Sorry I brought it up." She made a move to get up, but Jake put a hand on her shoulder, stopping her.

"Don't go yet."

"I should…I need to do..."

Her hesitancy gave him a small measure of hope as to ho

"Important things?" he gave her a loose smile.

She paused, then returned his smile and sat down again. "Not really."

The only sound in the ensuing quiet was the jingle of Pinto's bridle and the munching of grass as he grazed.

"You don't have crop to put in?"

"I do. In fact, I was supposed to finish seeding here, but I'm waiting for a part for the tractor."

Silence again.

"What were you going to—"

"How is the land sale—"

They both stopped at the same time, started again, then stopped again.

Miriam flashed him a quick smile. "I'll go first. Anita came by yesterday and took pictures, all apologetic that she hadn't come sooner. I'm okay with that."

"Why?"

Miriam just shrugged, looking around the property as if going back in time. "Sitting in New York, making these plans, seemed easier. But now that I'm here…" She let the sentence trail off, as if unsure of her decision.

Which ignited a tiny flicker of hope.

"Would you change your mind? About selling?"

Miriam looked pensive, and for a moment her hesitancy hovered, creating cautious hopes.

Which were extinguished with a firm shake of her head. "No. I can't."

He wanted nothing more than to push that but also could see from the set of her mouth, he would get nowhere. "But despite the memories of living here, you still seem content."

She pulled her knees close, wrapping her arms around them, her eyes roving over the land, her expression soft, welcoming. "I love it here."

Again, the question rose up, but he quenched it. Instead, he decided to take another angle. "I know I'm glad you're back. It's been good to see you."

A wary look flickered in her eyes, but then she drew in a

long, slow breath, granting him another smile. "It's been good to see you too."

He took a chance, moved closer. "Miriam, I feel like things are changing between us—"

"Don't, Jake," she said, holding out her hand to stop him. "Don't go there—"

He understood her reluctance, but a part of him couldn't let go. He'd gone through all they had been through to get to this moment. He knew he couldn't mess this up again. "I'm sorry, but I have to, Miriam. I don't have a lot of time with you, and you need to hear this."

"Please stop. You're making this too hard."

"What am I making too hard?" Jake let his hand linger on her shoulder, his fingers lightly caressing her neck. He didn't dare let go of her but didn't dare make more than this light connection.

She drew in one shaky breath and then another. "I've fought this feeling of unworthiness for many years. I don't like feeling this way, but I do. I do around you."

Jake heard her words, felt the pain pouring out of her. He didn't know what to say or how to say it.

"I know how that feels. I used to feel the same. But I've learned that my worth is not in who I am, but in who I trust. And I trust God to give me my worth. Not my bank account, or my land, or my job."

She said nothing to that, and he wondered if he had struck a chord.

"I've made some truly bad mistakes," she murmured, and Jake's heart skipped a beat, wondering what those could be.

But he kept his hand on her neck, maintained the connection. This was Miriam. The only woman he'd truly ever loved.

"I'm sure they're no worse than many others."

Another beat of silence. "No. But they have huge repercussions."

"Tell me."

She closed her eyes, then lowered her head. She gave him no answer.

He wanted her to trust him, tell him, but he also sensed that, unlike him, she'd been on her own so long, it was probably something she didn't know how to do anymore. All he could do was give her what he could.

He bent over and lightly touched his lips to her exposed neck. "I love you, Miriam," he whispered. "Always remember that."

And then he left.

Chapter 10

*M*iriam waited until she heard the soft footfalls of Jake's horse receding down the driveway.

Only then did she dare lift her head. She had come so close to releasing her secret shame. Years of keeping every thought to herself, every opinion, had honed her secrecy to an art. In her line of work, you learned the walls had ears and anything you said was repeated, changed, adjusted, then thrown back.

So, she had always kept her comments to a minimum. Never talked to the press. Never badmouthed anybody.

Always said as little as possible.

But oh, how she wanted to tell Jake everything. But did she dare? What they had been nurturing was growing—she'd be a fool not to realize that—but it was so fragile yet.

She was so afraid that telling him everything would make her lose him again.

With a gentle sigh, she lifted her hands to her neck, reliving the memory of his lips there, the peace she felt in his arms.

He had offered her his love. And she knew she couldn't take it. She had nothing to give him. Nothing.

Restless, she stood, brought the Bible she'd been reading back into the house. Did some busy work, tidying up a few more boxes. Setting them aside to be tossed out.

She wanted to talk to Tilly, but she had to make sure Jake wouldn't be there.

A quick phone call told her that Tilly was home. Jake was gone to town to pick up his tractor part. She had time.

Miriam jumped in her car and sped over. She could think of no one better to talk to than the woman who had been more than a mother to her.

Tilly was rolling out pie crusts on the kitchen counter when Miriam came into the house. Taryn was playing with scraps of leftover dough on the kitchen table—much as Miriam used to when she was younger. It looked so delightfully normal and was a welcome contrast to the turmoil she had just felt.

"I made a duck," Taryn announced to Miriam, showing her a roll of dough. "And some snakes. They're really easy to make."

Miriam stopped to admire the handiwork, unable to keep herself from stroking Taryn's head. She felt a connection with Jake when she spent time with his child.

Then she joined Tilly. "Need any help?"

Tilly smiled up at her. "You can get the filling ready. I'm making some lemon pies for the picnic tomorrow. Are you going to go?"

"Yes, I am."

"I've got all the things ready for the filling. You can start making it for me, if you want." Tilly pointed with her chin as she formed the pie crusts.

Miriam pulled out a pot from one cupboard and a wooden spoon from the drawer. While Miriam worked, Tilly slid the pie shells in the oven, set the timer, and began cleaning up.

"My goodness, I feel like quite the domestic," Miriam said

with a grin, as Tilly wiped the counter. The filling was just starting to boil, and she turned the heat off.

"You know," Tilly said, turning and leaning back against the counter, "it seems like just a short while ago that it was the last time you were standing at that stove, helping me make pie."

"I certainly came over here a lot," Miriam said, carefully licking the warm filling off the spoon. She set the pan aside for the filling to cool.

"Can I lick the spoon?" Taryn asked, looking up from her ducks and worms.

"Oops." Miriam looked at the now-clean wooden spoon and then at Taryn's crestfallen face. She had started licking the spoon completely out of habit. Turning, she washed the spoon, stuck it in the filling again, and brought it over to Taryn. "Be careful, honey. It's still a bit warm."

"Thanks, Miriam." Taryn took the spoon from her, touched her finger to it, and put it in her mouth. "I love lemon pie."

"So do I. It's still my favorite, and your grandma makes the best."

When the crusts were done, Miriam poured the filling into them while Tilly whipped up the egg whites. Soon, the counter held four tempting lemon pies.

Fred joined them then, still looking haggard.

"How are you feeling, Fred?" Miriam asked, concerned at his lack of color.

"Not great, my girl. Not great." He eased himself into his usual chair and caught his breath. "Whew. I guess I won't be running any sack races at the church picnic tomorrow, hey, Pipper?" he asked Taryn.

"Oh, Grandpa, you're silly," Taryn said, lining up her dough ducks. She showed her grandfather what she had made, and he was suitably impressed.

Tilly had made tea, and moments later, they were sitting

around the table, talking about all the wonderfully inconsequential things that make up a day.

Miriam felt herself relax in this comfortable home. It did that to her, she thought, taking a sip of her tea. Every time she came here, it was like coming home. She could pretend that Tilly was her mother, Fred her father.

And Taryn...

Miriam glanced sidelong at the little girl, who was busily playing with her dough animals. She resisted the urge to smooth the child's hair, to pull her close.

Jake's child.

Jake, who had told her he loved her. Told her that God loved her. And what was she supposed to do about that? What could she do? She had obligations, responsibilities she could not get out of.

Her debt on the business was adding up each month as the interest mounted. She needed the work Carl had lined up for her. It wouldn't get rid of all the debt, but it would be a good start. The sale of the farm would make the biggest difference. But it didn't look like that was happening real soon. So, she really needed the work Carl had found for her and more, which meant she needed to be thinking about going back to New York.

Not yet. Not yet, she thought.

When it was time for her to leave, it was time for her to think about all of that.

"What's the matter, Miriam?" Tilly asked. "You look troubled."

Miriam glanced up at Tilly, surprised at her perception. "I'm okay," she said evasively.

She forced her thoughts to the present. Forced herself to ask Taryn if she learned anything new in play school. Forced herself to ask Fred how the seeding was coming, hoping that maybe they would talk about Jake.

They didn't disappoint her.

She knew it was foolish to put herself through this, but she couldn't stop herself.

Eventually, the gentle chime of the grandfather clock in the living room reminded her of the time.

"Stay for supper, Miriam," Tilly said, frowning at her. "You don't have to leave right away."

But she did. Because if she stayed, she would see Jake, and right now her emotions were too fragile to deal with him.

So, she got up and promised Taryn again that she would come to the picnic.

"Can you take me in your car?" Taryn asked as Miriam was putting her shoes on the porch. "I never had a ride in your car."

"Yes, you did," Miriam said, pulling on her jacket. "I gave you a ride when we brought supper to your dad."

"But can I have another ride? Please?"

Miriam was about to say no but could really find no reason.

"Okay. I'll pick you up in the morning. You be ready, missy."

Taryn frowned. "Missy? I'm not missy. I'm Pipper. *You're* missy."

Miriam felt her throat catch at that. It was true. Fred always called her Missy. It would be like Taryn to notice that.

"Okay, Pipper. I'll come tomorrow. On time."

"Okeydokey." Taryn flashed Miriam a grin, and Miriam couldn't help but smile back.

She stuck her head through the doorway to say goodbye to Fred—

He was lying back in his chair at the table, his eyes closed, his mouth slightly open.

"Are you okay, Fred?" Miriam asked, panic slicing through her.

"Yeah, I am. Just resting," he said, lifting his head. He gave her a smile, but it looked forced.

"You sure?"

"Yes. I'm fine."

Tilly came to the door and gave her a quick kiss. "You stop by tomorrow after the picnic, you hear?"

Miriam hesitated, unsure of what tomorrow would bring.

"You come now, Miriam."

"Okay. I will."

She could get through this. She could.

"CAN my daddy have a ride in your car?" Taryn asked when Miriam came to the door on Sunday. She was sitting on a chair in the kitchen, trying to buckle up her shoes.

The thought of Jake sitting with her all the way to church was enough to make Miriam stop breathing. She tried to find a tactful way to forestall Taryn.

"I have to take my truck, Pipper," Jake said as he came into the kitchen. "I have to take some tables to the meadow for the picnic."

Miriam looked up at him as he stopped by the kitchen table to take a quick sip from his coffee. His hair was still damp from his shower, shining in the lights from the ceiling. His cheeks were freshly shaven, and she caught the faint scent of his after-shave lotion. It made her stomach flip.

He caught her eye, lifted his mouth in a careful smile, and walked toward her. She knew he was thinking of yesterday, of their time sitting together on her lawn while he read to her.

She hadn't been able to get him out of her mind. Somehow, though, it all seemed too good to be true.

"Will I see you at the picnic, Miriam?" Jake asked, holding his mug, leaning one hip against the door to the porch.

She swallowed at his nearness and could only nod. "Yeah. I promised Taryn and Donna I would go."

"Lucky Taryn," he said, and Miriam glanced up. She had

intended to look away right away but was unable to. Then Jake smiled again and turned to help his daughter.

"I'll see you at church, Pipper," he said, dropping a kiss on her head. "And I guess I'll see you, too," he said to Miriam.

Miriam nodded, caught Taryn's outstretched hand, and walked out to her car.

Luckily for her, she didn't have to say anything on the way to church. Taryn supplied all the conversation.

They pulled up in front of the church. *What a difference a week makes*, she thought, slowly getting out of the car. Last week, she had come here defensive, unwilling and unready to be a part of this community.

During the week, she had met up with old friends, had reconnected with the community. Had spent time with Fred and Tilly. Taryn.

Had found out the truth about Jake and Paula.

She glanced over her shoulder at the graveyard, wondering about Paula. Wondering how Paula had thought she could build a marriage on a lie.

Miriam turned away from Paula and the past, and, pulling her long skirt close to her, closed her car door. Today was Sunday. A day of renewal and blessing. She wasn't going to let the past and its mistakes overshadow it.

Taryn bounced up the sidewalk, then, at the sound of a truck engine, stopped. Miriam turned around.

Jake pulled up beside her car.

Miriam waited, feeling slightly foolish, as Taryn went running back to her father, her cheeks flushed, her ponytail bobbing. "You have to sit with me and Miriam."

Jake smiled down at Taryn, then looked up at Miriam. He stood beside them, his expression enigmatic. Then, as their eyes met, she saw his mouth lift in a crooked smile.

And her heart did that funny little dance.

Taryn caught her hand and Jake's as they walked toward the church.

It felt right, Miriam thought with a gentle ache. It felt as if this was how it should be.

As they walked up the stairs, Miriam looked once again at Jake and was unnerved by his direct gaze.

"I didn't have a chance to ask how you are doing, Miriam," he said. His voice was quiet, but it carried a wealth of meaning. Miriam knew he alluded to yesterday and was suddenly shy.

"I'm glad to be here," she said, looking away. Which was the truth. She was not entirely comfortable yet but still glad to be a part of this.

Through the thin material of her shirt, she felt the warm weight of his callused hand resting on her shoulder. She swallowed at the contact, resisting the urge to lift her shoulder to hold his hand against her cheek.

"That's good," he said, squeezing ever so slightly.

"Daddy, why did you let go of my hand?" Taryn demanded.

Miriam felt her cheeks flush and was surprised at her reaction. She hadn't felt this flustered around a man since—her heart lifted again—since she and Jake had first started dating.

"Where's Tilly and Fred?" Miriam asked, finally noticing their absence.

"Dad is really tired so Mom thought it would be better if she stayed home with him."

"I'm sorry," Miriam said, holding his gaze. She couldn't look away, couldn't break the contact.

"Miriam, good to see you." Donna breezed up beside her, and Jake drew away. Miriam tried not to feel disappointed and turned to her friend.

Donna gave her a quick hug, smiling as she pulled away. "Hello, Jake," she said as her gaze flicked to Jake and then back to Miriam. To her credit, Donna's expression remained neutral, although when she looked back at Miriam, she gave just a hint of a wink.

Donna smiled down at Taryn. "Bet your grandma made lemon pie again, didn't she?"

Taryn nodded, beaming up at Donna. "We brought three. And Miriam helped make them."

"Three lemon pies? And Miriam helped make them?" Donna raised her eyebrows exaggeratedly. "My goodness. We are getting domestic, aren't we?"

Miriam laughed. The thump of many small footsteps coming up the steps behind them made Donna turn.

"Here comes my tribe, and there goes the peace. I'll talk to you later."

Miriam watched as Donna became surrounded by a noisy group of children. Donna licked her finger and smoothed down a cowlick on one, straightened the collar of another and picked up a little girl. Her husband joined her and took the girl from her. Then they all walked into the church.

"Sort of makes you feel breathless, doesn't she?" Jake asked as they watched Donna's family walk down the aisle.

"She always had a lot of energy," Miriam said.

"I heard you had a girls' afternoon out with her."

Miriam glanced at him again. Again, he was smiling.

"Yes. I had a nice afternoon catching up with old friends."

"I'm glad," he said, and Miriam wondered what he meant.

"Let's go," Taryn said, tugging on Miriam's hand.

They walked down the aisle of the church as a threesome. But this time, Miriam felt less like a stranger and more like a part of things. One of her old friends glanced up as they passed and waggled her fingers at her. Another raised her eyebrows and winked.

Because the church was full, Jake ended up sitting directly beside Miriam, with Taryn on his lap.

Miriam tried to still the nervous thumping of her heart at his nearness. This was foolish, she rebuked herself. A person shouldn't be feeling this in church.

She pulled a Bible out of the pew and started to read it, trying to concentrate on the words. But Taryn kept chattering to her, and Miriam had to respond.

Then the minister came in, the worship service began, and Miriam felt as if all the loose pieces of her life were being shaken around.

She paid close attention to the songs, searching. It was as if she were on the edge of something important, earth-shattering—but she couldn't quite grasp it.

This was a good place to be, she thought, as she sang along with the hymns. She had missed so much by staying away from church all those years.

And yet, as the service progressed, she knew there should be more. This wasn't just a comfortable tradition that made people feel good. There was a sense of worship and awe, and Miriam knew she hadn't quite caught it yet. It gave her a sense of disappointment and yet, at the same time, an eagerness to find out for herself what was missing.

It seemed as if the service was over too quickly.

She had managed not to concentrate too much on Jake. Taryn had fallen asleep on his shoulder, and he had held her. Once he had laid his arm along the back of the pew behind her. It had been hard to concentrate then, but she had managed.

THE ORGAN BURST into the postlude, and with a gentle sigh Miriam turned.

Jake barred her way, still holding a sleeping Taryn. "Enjoy the service?"

"Yes. I did," she replied, returning his direct gaze.

He smiled and nodded, touching her arm lightly. "I'm so glad."

Then Taryn woke up, someone jostled Miriam from behind, and the moment was broken.

Somehow, they got separated in the flow of people leaving the sanctuary. Miriam met up with Donna and a few of her old friends. They told her where the picnic was, and when Miriam got to her car, she noted with dismay that Jake was gone. She had been kind of hoping Taryn would want a ride to the picnic in her car.

She felt a sharp stab of disappointment, then shook it off. She had just experienced a wonderful Sunday, and she was going to enjoy the church picnic, something she hadn't attended since leaving Waylen.

And she was looking forward to being with Jake because she also knew that once they were there, he would make sure they would spend some time together.

Her heart hitched. She didn't want to think further than this afternoon. It was a special time, a gift. The future was for another day.

"WHERE'S MIRIAM, DADDY?" Taryn tugged on Jake's arm. "She has to eat her pie."

"I'm sure she's here somewhere." Jake frowned as he looked around. He had left right after church and had insisted Taryn come with him. She had pouted but had given in.

"I wanna play with my friends," Taryn announced to Jake. He nodded, then looked around for someone to visit with.

He ended up in a group of men talking about the usual topics that take up a farmer's mind—the crops, the weather, the prices of their commodities. They stood around, a short distance from the tables being set with food, their stances identical—hands in their pockets, occasional comments punctuating the conversation.

Jake could hold his own in these situations. Once he had started farming, he knew it was the only thing he wanted to do. He loved the routine of the life, the ebb and flow of the seasons. It hadn't taken him long to establish his own position in the community. He often wished he had been able to go to school, to further his knowledge, but farmers were an independent lot, intensely involved in their own operations. There was always some seminar being offered at any given time, and Jake went to each one.

"Put any canola in this year, Jake?" one of the men asked him.

"No, Andrew. I seeded the Spencer quarters to it last year. I thought I would hold off this year."

"I heard the Spencer land is up for sale. Aren't you interested?"

Jake shrugged the comment away. "I'm stretched to the limit."

"Aw, c'mon. I know old Fred. He's got some stashed away, I'm sure." Andrew nudged Jake with an elbow, his eyebrows raised lightly as if to negate Jake's comment.

"I'm not taking any chances with money that isn't mine."

"Is it true Miriam's heading back east?" another asked him.

Jake loved this community, but privacy was a luxury not given its members.

"She has other obligations," he said casually.

"Too bad. Didn't the two of you have something going, once upon a time?"

Jake laughed lightly. "That was a long time ago, Andrew." For a relationship that was supposed to be a huge secret, a lot of people not only knew about it but also remembered it. Ten years later.

"Speaking of Miriam, there she is."

Jake tried not to turn too fast. Tried to keep his heart from jumping around like a frisky calf. He managed a semblance of nonchalance by waiting and then glancing over his shoulder.

She stood in the middle of a bunch of her old friends, talking animatedly. As she spoke, she gestured with her hands, graceful movements that emphasized her delicate bone structure. She wore a loose T-shirt and full skirt in vibrant earth colors that brought out highlights in her short brown hair and set off the peach tone of her skin.

Her beauty made his chest tighten, and he wondered again how he could think she would even be interested in him.

An errant breeze lifted a strand of her hair and dropped it across her eyes. As she lifted her hand to brush it away, she looked up.

And straight at him.

Her gentle smile caught at him as a connection was made that excluded everyone else. There was no one around but the two of them. He saw no one but her.

We belong together, he thought, then remembered to breathe. The sound of laughter permeated the moment. Miriam's neighbor caught her arm. Andrew asked Jake another question, and the interval was swept away.

Jake felt his life shift, saw this possibility as attainable. Miriam here, with him. He knew that this moment was a hint of what could be.

He smiled as he thought of the rest of the afternoon. Taryn would be busy. Her friends would find other people to talk to. He hoped sometime, somewhere, he could get Miriam alone.

A truck pulled up, and Jake was coerced into unloading a few more tables for more food. He caught scattered glimpses of Miriam as the tables were organized—warm dishes, still-steaming plates of soft buns, bowls of colorful salads, pans of dessert.

Then, at an unseen signal, families began gathering, parents bending over to put food on their children's plates. Small hands pointing, heads shaking their emphatic "no."

Jake looked for Taryn and then saw her. With Miriam.

He smiled, watching as Taryn made Miriam lift lids off casseroles. It wasn't difficult to tell which of the dishes met with her favor and which didn't. Miriam patiently worked her way along the table and once glanced up at Jake. She smiled, then looked down again.

Jake waited until the families had served their children and took his own place in the lineup. When his plate was full, he looked about for his daughter. She and Miriam had found a place under a tree and were already starting.

Jake sauntered over, nodding his greetings to people who called out to him but not allowing himself to get waylaid.

"We prayed already, Daddy," Taryn said, looking up at him with cheeks already smeared with tomato sauce. "And I found s'getti."

"I see that." Jake pulled out his handkerchief and squatted down, trying to wipe her cheeks with one hand, balance his plate of food with the other.

"Here. I'll do that." Miriam took the handkerchief from him and wiped the worst of the sauce off, while Taryn tried to help by licking her cheeks. "There. That looks a little better."

She frowned at Taryn. "Are you feeling okay? You feel a bit warm."

Taryn shook her head. "I'm not sick."

"I didn't say you were sick, just warm. You looked flushed, too!"

"Nope, I'm good," Taryn insisted. "I have to run races."

"It is warm out," Jake said, balancing his warm plate on his lap. Then with a quick glance at Miriam, he bent his head.

He thanked the Lord for the beautiful day, for having Miriam and Taryn with him. He prayed for his father and his mother. Then, almost hesitantly, he prayed that Miriam would be willing to stay. That they could rediscover what they had missed all those years ago.

With a soft sigh, he looked up. Miriam was toying with her fork, pushing around some pasta, a light frown on her face.

"What's the matter, Miriam?"

She looked up at him, her eyes wide, then shook her head. "Nothing," she replied. "Nothing at all."

Jake ate slowly, surprised to find his appetite had decreased. He managed to eat it all, but by the time he was done, Taryn was restless.

"I wanna go with my friends," she said, standing up. "I wanna go in the races."

"You didn't finish your spaghetti," Miriam said.

"I'm not hungry."

"Let's go then," Miriam said, slowly getting up.

"We'll go together." Jake wiped his mouth, balled up the paper napkin, and got up. They deposited their paper plates and plastic utensils in a garbage can and walked over to where young children were already gathering for the annual races.

Taryn pulled away from them, running over to be with her friends, leaving Jake and Miriam on the sidelines.

"I guess we'll have to cheer her on," Miriam said, glancing up at Jake with a grin.

"She expects it." Jake looked down at her, hoping he appeared nonchalant. She glanced up at him, then away, biting her lip. He wondered if she felt the same way he did.

Jake felt guilty because, much as he loved his daughter, right now, he didn't want to stand beside Miriam and watch Taryn race. Right now, he wanted to take Miriam to some-place private, pull her into his arms…

"You have to watch me, Daddy," Taryn called out.

Jake blinked and shook his head to rein in his own drifting thoughts.

He looked at his daughter and couldn't help but grin. Taryn was bent over at the waist, her elbows up, fists balled at her sides, in an exaggerated runner's stance. Someone called out "Ready, set" and then "go," and Taryn was off, legs pumping, arms swinging, her face screwed up in a tight frown.

"Pretty intense, isn't she?" Miriam said, laughing.

"She stays focused."

Miriam nodded, crossing her arms over her stomach and shivering lightly.

"Cold?" Jake asked.

"No."

They were silent again, watching as Taryn came walking back to them, her head hanging.

"I didn't win, Daddy," she said with a pout. "I runned my fastest, and I didn't win."

Jake crouched down and gave her a quick hug. "That's okay. I watched you run. You went real fast. You don't have to win for it to be fun."

But Taryn wasn't convinced by the platitudes. She stayed beside Jake and Miriam for the second race, complaining of a headache, but by the time they announced the sack race, she was game again.

This time, she won. And this time, she was all smiles. She came back with a red ribbon and a huge grin on her face.

"I wonned. I wonned." She waved the ribbon.

"Wow, that's a pretty ribbon." Donna had come up and was now crouched beside Taryn, admiring the ribbon. She glanced up at Jake with a knowing smile. "Do you mind if I take Taryn off your hands for a while? My kids are going to get their faces painted, and then we're going to do some old-fashioned apple bobbing."

Jake could have hugged her. "No. Not at all."

Donna winked at Miriam, then took Taryn's hand and walked away.

Jake felt as nervous as he had on his very first date with Miriam. He didn't quite know what to say, how to go about this whole dating thing.

"So, looks like she'll be busy for a while," he said inanely.

Miriam nodded, avoiding his gaze.

Jake tried to think of something else to say. Something that wouldn't sound fake, fatuous. Finally, he decided the straight-forward approach was the best.

"Let's go for a walk, Miriam. I want to talk to you."

Miriam glanced at him over her shoulder, her eyes wide. "Okay," she said.

Jake took her arm and studiously avoided the glances of the people close by them. They walked up the hill, through the long grass, until they came to a quiet grove of trees. It was cooler in there, and Jake saw Miriam shiver again. He glanced over his shoulder, but they were still in plain sight, so they walked a little farther.

Finally, he couldn't stand it any longer. He caught her by the arm and turned her around.

"I think we're far enough now," he said quietly, pulling her into his arms as he leaned back against a convenient tree.

She came willingly, slipping her arms around his waist, laying her head against his chest.

Jake sighed and pulled her close, resting his head on hers. He rubbed his cheek along its soft silkiness, over and over again.

"I love you, Miriam. You know that."

Her only reply was a careful nod.

"So, now what?"

She didn't move, didn't reply, only held him more tightly.

Jake bent and brushed his lips over her shoulder, then nudged her head aside with his chin. She looked up at him. Their faces were so close, he could feel her breath, could feel the warmth of her burning cheeks.

And then he kissed her.

It was like coming home after a hard day. It was like a drink of water after a long thirst.

They belonged together, and as he kissed her, it was as if she had never left. That familiar touch, taste, and feel. She felt right in his arms, as no other woman ever had.

Her lips were cool and soft, and as his mouth moved over

hers, he reached up to stroke her cheek, run his fingers through her hair.

She murmured his name, caressing his shoulders.

Reluctantly, he pulled away. With his forefinger, he traced the exquisite line of her eyebrow, the softness of her cheek, her lips.

She closed her eyes as he touched her, her hands tightening on his waist.

"What are you doing to me, Jake?" she sighed.

"Trying to show you what you mean to me." He pulled her close again, content just to hold her. He knew she hadn't made any declaration to him and wondered if she would. He didn't want to force anything out of her, but his own heart ached to hear something—some kind of confirmation of how she felt. He knew she felt something. She wouldn't have let him hold her, kiss her, if she didn't.

He just wished he knew what.

"Jake, tell me. Tell me in words."

He heard a yearning in her voice and wondered if she was even aware of it. "I love you more the longer you stay here." He touched her hair, his fingers playing with the soft waves. "I'm not that good with words. But when you're with me, I feel like all the things that were missing are here. I feel like holding you is what I was meant to do from the moment I was born. That this is part of my purpose in life."

She slipped her cheek over his shirt, a light caressing move.

"Jake," she said softly. That was all. Just his name, but it held much more. She drew back, still holding him. She looked deep into his eyes, then her gaze traveled over his face, as if memorizing it. "You're the only man I ever loved. Ever."

Her words rocked through him, taking his breath away.

"I know it sounds silly," she continued. "But it's true. I had to tell you."

"Oh, Miriam. Do you know how long I've waited to hear

you say those words?" He wanted to kiss her again, wanted to shout the news to the world. "I think I've waited long enough. I have to ask you. Will you marry me?"

He felt a tremor in her arms as she clung to him. Her eyes opened wide and then slowly shut. She shook her head.

"Not that, Jake. Not that."

"What do you mean?" He felt as if all the breath had been pressed from him. He had just opened his heart to her, made himself as vulnerable as he had ever done with any woman, and now she sounded as if she hadn't wanted to hear it.

She caught him around his neck and pulled his head down to hers, kissing him hard. For a moment, he let her. For a moment, he pretended that she returned his feelings for her. But then, sensing her confusion, he carefully drew away.

"Miriam, what's wrong?"

She said nothing, only laid her head against his chest again. "Nothing."

He knew better but also sensed that, for now, he didn't want to explore her reticence. She was in his arms. She had said nothing about his proposal. It still hung between them, and he didn't dare bring it up again. He felt a shiver of panic, wondering if she was still figuring on leaving tomorrow.

He didn't want to think about it. He remembered how willingly she had come into his arms. Remembered that she had told him she loved him, too.

She shivered, and Jake straightened. The moment had passed, and nothing had happened. Disappointment crushed him, and he could say nothing to her as they walked back.

People were grouped together, visiting. Some were watching the little children getting their faces painted. Somehow, on their way back, Miriam drifted away from him, and Jake let her go.

He was confused and hurt and didn't know where to go from there. Okay, Lord. I opened my heart to her, told her exactly what my intentions were. Help me to understand what is happening. Work in her heart. I know she needs to be here. I know she belongs here. Help her to see that.

Jake wanted to leave right away, but Taryn was getting her face painted, and he knew it would look very rude if he suddenly left. So, he hung around, made meaningless conversation, and all the while tried not to look out for Miriam.

Chapter 11

"There you are."

Miriam turned with a start to face her friend, Donna.

"Taryn's not feeling well," Donna said, frowning. "She's been asking for you."

"Where's Jake?" Miriam didn't want to go. She didn't want to run the risk of seeing Jake so soon after turning down his proposal.

"I can't find him. I thought he'd be with you. Besides, it's you she wants. C'mon." Donna tugged on her arm, and glancing around one more time, Miriam followed.

"But she was fine just half an hour ago." *A lifetime ago*, she thought.

"I wouldn't worry about it, Miriam. Goodness, you sound like a guilty mother." Donna nudged her in the side. "I know exactly what you were doing. You don't need to look so guilty."

Miriam couldn't stop the flush that warmed her cheeks. It was as if everyone here knew exactly what had happened for that short while that she and Jake had disappeared.

She felt her stomach tighten at the thought of his

proposal. What was she supposed to do now? How could she go back to New York, how could she continue a life that she disliked, knowing that everything she wanted was here—but how could she stay and accept Jake's proposal? How could she make her financial problems his? She couldn't.

"What's the matter, Miriam? You look so sad."

Miriam was tempted to tell her. But she had spent too many years taking care of herself, and confessions didn't come easily to her.

"I'm okay. I'm just worried about Taryn," she lied.

"Well, she's just over here, lying down." Donna brought Miriam to where Taryn lay, curled up on a blanket. She sat up when Miriam approached, and Miriam could see how flushed her cheeks were, past the bright flowers painted on them.

"What's the matter, Pipper?" Miriam asked, crouching down at the little girl's side.

"My head hurts again."

Miriam laid a hand on her forehead and was surprised to feel how hot it was. "But you seemed fine this morning," she said aloud. Then she remembered how the child had slept on Jake's lap in church. That wasn't normal for Taryn. That much, Miriam knew.

"I'll go get Jake. He might want to take her home," Donna said, getting up.

Miriam sat down and drew Taryn onto her lap, cradling her warm body close. What had she done, leaving her like this, going off with Jake like some teenager? How could she be so irresponsible?

She's not my little girl, she thought. Miriam stroked Taryn's hair back from her face. It didn't matter. She shouldn't have left.

Taryn said nothing, just lay there, adding to Miriam's guilt. Then Jake rushed to her side, falling down on one knee beside them. He also laid his hand on Taryn's forehead and met Miriam's eyes.

"I feel terrible," Miriam said. "She just doesn't feel well."

"Let me take her. I think she'd better go home."

Taryn protested as Jake tried to take her away from Miriam's arms. "No. I want Miriam." The little girl clung to Miriam, and there was nothing she could do.

Jake helped Miriam up and tried once more, unsuccessfully, to make Taryn go to him.

"I'll bring her to your truck," Miriam said.

"I wanna go in your car. You said so." Taryn lifted her head, her expression downcast. "I wanna go in your car."

Miriam didn't know why Taryn was being so stubborn. A combination of not feeling well and just plain Taryn, she figured.

"I used my truck to bring the tables here," Jake said as they walked down to where they had parked the vehicles. "I imagine they'll need it to bring them back to the church."

"I'll get my husband to bring your truck to your place," Donna offered. "Why don't you just get Taryn home. We'll make sure your truck gets back."

Jake shot her a grateful smile and turned back to Miriam. "So, we'll take your car, then, if that's okay?"

"Fine. Of course." She shifted Taryn so that the child was easier to hold.

They walked slowly down to the car, Jake beside Miriam, supporting her as they walked. She hadn't realized how heavy Taryn was. When they got to the car, Jake took the keys from her, unlocked her door, and helped her in.

Then he got in on the driver's side, and they were off. They drove in silence.

Miriam couldn't look at him, but she was remembering his declaration of love. His proposal. She closed her eyes, laying her head on Taryn's, unable to think of the implications of what he had said to her.

By the time they got to Fred and Tilly's house, Taryn was asleep again, her body burning up with fever. This time, Jake took her from Miriam and carried her into the house. Miriam followed behind.

Tilly was sleeping in the recliner when they walked through the living room on their way upstairs. She sat up with a jolt when she saw them.

"What's the matter?" She got up, rubbing her eyes.

"Taryn's not feeling good," Jake said tersely as he strode up the stairs.

"She feels like she has a fever," Miriam added, waiting for Tilly to join her. Together, they went upstairs.

Jake was stripping Taryn out of her clothes and putting her in her pajamas. "She's just burning up," Jake said, slipping the nightgown over her head.

"Let's take her temperature." Tilly walked to the bathroom and found a thermometer. She cleaned it, then shook it as she brought it back to the bedroom. Taryn was sitting up, her eyes looking glazed, her cheeks a vivid red.

"Here, honey, open up." Tilly put the thermometer in her mouth, and the three adults waited.

Miriam felt slightly out of place, standing here, but she didn't want to go. She felt partially responsible, even though common sense told her that Taryn had probably already been coming down with this bug last night.

Tilly took the thermometer out and tried to read it. She handed it to Jake, who read out, "One hundred and three."

"That's high," Miriam said, chewing her lip. "Shouldn't we give her something for that?"

"I have some children's medication we can give her," Tilly said, sighing lightly. "Jake, you go downstairs and get a spoon for me." When they left, Miriam sat down beside Taryn, who was fretting.

"My head is sore, Miriam. How come my head is sore?"

"You have a fever. That means there's something bad in your blood, and the good cells are fighting it. That's why you're hot."

Taryn nodded and curled up on the bed. "I'm tired."

"Your grandma is getting you something that will help take down the fever," Miriam said, stroking her hair away from her forehead. Just then, Tilly came in the room with a bottle and a glass of water, and Jake came with a spoon. Miriam took the bottle and measured out the dosage according to the instructions on the bottle. "Here, open wide."

Taryn obeyed and then pulled a face. She grabbed for the glass of water and gulped it down. Then, with a sigh, she lay down again.

Miriam adjusted the blankets around her, as Jake pulled the blinds down over the window. Miriam stroked Taryn's cheek once and then left.

Tilly took the medicine back to the bathroom, then followed Jake and Miriam down the stairs. Back in the living room, she dropped into her recliner. "Oh, Jake, Simon called. Said it was important. He'll call you again tonight."

"What did he want?"

"Didn't say."

"How's Dad?" Jake asked.

Tilly just shook her head. "Not good. I don't know what to do. I might have to take him to the doctor again tomorrow."

"You look tired, Tilly."

"I am." She sighed and closed her eyes again.

Miriam sat down on the couch and couldn't help but glance at the clock. She was shocked to see that it was already five o'clock—almost suppertime. "What did you have for lunch, Tilly?"

"I didn't feel like making lunch."

Miriam glanced at Jake, then got up. "I'll get some supper together for you. I'm sure Fred should have something."

"He says he's not hungry."

Miriam heard the note of despair in her voice and walked to her side. She bent over and kissed Tilly lightly. "I'll see what he wants, and I'll take care of it. You just sit here."

Tilly smiled up at her and caught her hand. "Thanks, child. You are special."

Miriam doubted that, but the words warmed her heart, anyway.

Fred was awake when she peeked into his bedroom. He looked haggard and worn. When Miriam asked if he wanted anything, he said no.

"What about some soup?"

"I don't know."

"I'm going to take that as a yes. And Jake is going to make sure you eat it all," she warned before she left the room.

Back in the kitchen, Miriam wondered what she had gotten herself into. She wanted to leave, but how could she with Fred and Taryn sick? So, Miriam found a recipe that she knew was Fred's favorite. It was also easy to make. Quick potato soup.

Luckily, there were some leftover potatoes in the fridge, and soon Miriam had the ingredients together and was adding them one at a time to the pot on the stove.

She was just stirring the grated cheese into the soup when she saw Jake leaning on the counter beside her. She didn't want to look at him but couldn't stop herself. How easy it was to lose herself in those eyes, to let herself drift toward him.

His hand on her arm stopped her, and she turned her attention back to the soup, stirring it as if everything important to her was in that pot.

Then he left her, and she breathed a sigh of relief. This wasn't turning out at all the way she had planned. She was supposed to be leaving tomorrow, and each encounter with Jake tested her resolve. She had no right to encourage him. But she was weak, lonely—and in love with a man she couldn't have. Shouldn't have.

Miriam swallowed, praying for strength. This isn't fair, Lord. This just isn't fair. To give him back to me and make him so unattainable at the same time.

Jake sat with Fred while he ate, and Tilly and Miriam sat in the kitchen. Taryn was sleeping, still fitfully. She would until the fever broke, Tilly informed Miriam.

Miriam knew absolutely nothing about childhood illnesses and was worried sick. She couldn't understand why neither Tilly nor Jake was sitting upstairs with her at this very minute.

The dishes were done, Tilly had gone to bed, and the medication Taryn had taken was starting to kick in when Miriam decided to go. She tidied up the living room, delaying the inevitable, yet knowing she was playing a dangerous game. She wanted to see Jake again.

He came downstairs after checking on Taryn, and when he saw her in the living room, he paused at the bottom of the stairs. "So, I guess you have to go?"

Miriam nodded, still clutching a newspaper she had found on the floor.

He shoved his hands through his hair and sighed. "I know this is going to sound terribly improper, but I have to leave early in the morning to finish seeding." He hesitated, biting his lip. "I was wondering if you would mind staying here tonight, just until Tilly gets up. I'm worried about Taryn..." He let the sentence trail off, and at that moment, Miriam could see utter weariness in his eyes.

"I'll stay, Jake."

"Thanks." His eyes met hers, and he slowly walked over.

He was going to kiss her, she knew that.

He didn't even touch her—just bent over, his lips lightly caressing hers.

"I still love you, Miriam. I want to marry you."

She laid a finger on his lips to forestall him, her heart contracting with pain. "Please, Jake. Don't make this any harder for me than it already is."

"Don't make what harder?"

"Leaving."

She saw the stricken look on his face. She lowered her

gaze as if to erase the memory, then felt his hands on her shoulders again.

"Jake." She couldn't stop herself. "I love you, I do. But I can't be what you want me to be." She felt her face twist with sorrow. "I can't be the kind of mother that Taryn needs. I thought I could, but when I saw Donna with her children, I realized how little I knew. I don't fit here." She drew in a shaky breath, curled her fingers around each other. What she said was partly true. But she couldn't tell him everything.

"Where do you fit, Miriam?" He asked the question softly as he drew her into his arms. "If you don't fit here, why do you think you'll fit in a place that you don't want to go back to? I know you don't. I see the look on your face when you talk about your work."

Miriam bit her lip, resisting the urge to lay her head on his chest, to let him take all her problems and fix them. But it would be putting even more on his shoulders than he already carried. It wasn't fair to him, and if she truly loved him, she would leave. She knew it was the only way.

Jake tightened his hold on her, caressed her head with his chin. "I won't stop loving you, Miriam. So, where does that leave me?"

He took a step back, lifted her chin with his finger, and laid a gentle kiss on her lips. "Think about that when you're heading back east."

Miriam swayed as he stepped back. She wrapped her arms about her waist again, her chin down. She couldn't look at him. Couldn't tell him. She knew how important his family was, this farm. It was the first place he had told her that he felt he belonged. She couldn't jeopardize that. If they were to get married, her debt would become his. It was too much.

Silence again. A dark, intense silence that kept them apart.

"I'll set out some towels for you," Jake said, then turned and left.

Miriam watched him go back upstairs, his tall figure disappearing from view. He didn't look back.

Confusion tortured her thoughts. She knew she had to stay. She couldn't leave tomorrow. Not with Fred so sick, Taryn not feeling well, and Tilly so exhausted. There was no way she could simply drive away and leave Jake to carry this.

But how could she stay? How could she see him every day, knowing she couldn't have him?

She dropped her head in her hands at the thought of being around Jake that long. So close and yet so far.

This isn't fair, Lord, she thought. I can't do this to him. The only thing I can do is leave. He will think I hate him, when I'm doing it because I love him.

She didn't know what to say, didn't know how to pray. She thought back to that morning, to the service, to yesterday and what Jake had told her.

It was too bewildering, and it was too early to go to bed. She dropped into the recliner and, glancing to the side, noticed the Bible. She needed comfort and guidance, and in these lonely hours of the night, she didn't know where else to turn.

She opened it and turned to Romans, the same chapter Jake had read from. Slowly, she reread the words, clinging to one love she knew she was allowed to claim.

She had lived a life close to God before. Would He take her back?

Nothing could separate her from God's love. The Bible said so. The same Bible that had brought good news to millions of people for hundreds of years. So many people before her believed it; many after her would, as well.

Miriam closed her eyes, her thoughts becoming prayers. Nothing, she thought. No present or future. Her past, her mistakes, her mother's mistakes, the things she wished she could change—none of that would separate her from the love of God shown in Christ. He would take her no matter what she came with. His love encompassed her regardless of her debt.

She reread the words again and again, and slowly she felt power surge through her. This wasn't a battle she had to fight alone. She didn't have the strength. All she had to do was take what was given. The other night, on the hillside, she had struggled, had tried to find God, as Jake had suggested.

She had gone about it all wrong, she realized, tracing the words of the passage with her finger. God was waiting for her to stop the struggle, to let Him give.

Miriam clutched the Bible, her eyes closing as she opened her tightly held heart and gave it over to God. She felt a joy and peace flood her heart. Tears of cleansing thankfulness drifted past her closed eyelids and down her cheeks as she found herself quietly humming songs from her youth. Songs of praise.

She opened the Bible again randomly and started reading John. She stopped at John 16:24. "Until now you have not asked for anything in my name. Ask and you will receive and your joy will be complete."

I want to do something for Jake, she prayed. That is all I ask. Something to show him I love him. Something he will remember. I know he loves me, and I know that leaving will seem like betrayal, but I can't ask that of him. I can't.

She read on, gaining strength and comfort. She knew she would need everything she could to get her through the next day—until she left.

"Thank you, Lord," she said quietly.

Everyone, except Jake, was still asleep by the time Miriam got up the next morning. She hadn't slept much. She was too aware of the fact that Jake lay only a room away from her. It made her edgy and nervous, and by the time she woke up again, she was sure she had gotten only a couple of hours' sleep. Jake's alarm woke her up. However, she waited until she heard the sound of the tractor leaving the yard before she rose.

She would have to wait until Tilly was up to run home for a fresh change of clothes.

She sat down in the recliner again and picked up the Bible. She read through some of the Psalms, again seeking and finding the comfort she had found last night. In the silence of the morning, she prayed again. Prayed for God's good and perfect will to make itself known to her.

Then, unable to sit any longer, she went upstairs and checked on Taryn. The child was still asleep, still feverish. But she didn't seem as warm as yesterday.

Miriam brushed the hair out of Taryn's face, lightly touching her cheek. Taryn sighed and turned onto her back, still sleeping.

Miriam felt a rush of tenderness for this young child and wished she could stay, prayed she could stay. I don't want lots of money, Lord. I don't need to be rich. If I could stay here, it would be all I'd want.

Miriam mentally pulled herself back from these lives that she had to leave soon. Turning, she left the room.

She cleaned up what she could and then went back downstairs to set the table for breakfast and possibly make a pot of tea for Tilly.

The shrill ring of the phone broke the silence of the house. Miriam almost ran to get it, snatched it off the hook. "Hello, Prins household," she said, breathless.

"This isn't Tilly, is it?"

"No."

"Don't tell me Jake got married without telling me?"

What a thing to say to a complete stranger! "I'm sorry. If you wish to speak to Jake, he's gone already," Miriam said, unable to keep the prim tone out of her voice.

"My goodness, you're a secretary. Since when does Jake need a secretary?" the man said with a laugh.

"May I ask who is calling?" Miriam asked.

"You may." Silence followed this comment, and then Miriam recognized the joke. And the voice.

"Hello, Simon," she said dryly.

"Wow. An amazing secretary who recognizes voices of someone she has never met. Who are you?"

"Miriam Spencer."

A pause followed that, as she sensed Simon trying to place her. "Okay," he said triumphantly. "Ah, yes. The high school fling."

Miriam knew she had been more to Jake than a fling but didn't deign to comment on that.

"Did he get my message last night?"

"Yes. Tilly told him you called."

"Well, this is kinda sudden, but I'm leaving right away for the airport. I'll be there sometime this afternoon. Do you know if he's done seeding yet?"

Miriam was confused. "As far as I know, he should be done today."

"Great. My timing is, as usual, impeccable. I know this is short notice, but I'm hoping to get there by about three. If Jake isn't home, then you and I can sit down, have tea, and you can remind me what a jerk I used to be."

"Okay." Miriam tried to keep her voice cool, remembering his unmerciful teasing whenever he would visit and how Jake had always intervened, standing up for Miriam.

"Well, take care," Simon said, his voice breezy, before hanging up.

As she hung up, she glanced at the clock, and, as if to force herself to stay on course, phoned Carl.

"So, you heading out today?" he asked.

"Well, something came up here. I'm probably leaving this afternoon."

"That's cutting it a bit close, but I guess you know your own limits. How are you feeling?"

In love. Confused. Scared. Forgiven. "I'm okay," she said.

"You don't sound okay."

"I'm fine. I've got to go. Talk to you later."

"Hey. Hang in there, girl. We'll untangle this financial business once you start working."

Not quick enough to make any difference here, she thought wryly. She knew she was looking at a minimum of four years of heavy payments, if she got other contracts as good as the one Carl had gotten for her. Otherwise it would be longer. "Yeah. It'll be fine."

Chapter 12

"*S*mells good in here."

Miriam turned from washing the dishes in the sink to see Tilly in the doorway, yawning. The woman had dark rings under her eyes; her skin was blotchy and puffy with fatigue. She drew her light blue bathrobe around her and blinked. Without her glasses, she looked especially vulnerable.

And old.

"Not a good night, Tilly?" Miriam asked, pulling out a chair for her. She had been busy in the kitchen, baking Fred's favorite muffins, hoping she could tempt his appetite.

"I felt like I didn't sleep, but I must have." She smiled her thanks as Miriam poured her a cup of tea from a carafe. It was still steaming.

Tilly caught the mug close to her, as if to absorb its warmth. "So. Leaving today?" Hard to miss the sorrow in Tilly's voice.

Hard not to feel guilty about it.

"Later on. I'm driving back so I can make up the time along the way."

Tilly took a careful sip of her tea and sighed. "How's Taryn?"

"She's sleeping well now. Not restless. She's still a bit warm. I don't know if she's feverish."

"The fever must have broken, or she'd still be hot." Tilly looked around the kitchen. "Thanks for cleaning up. And for making supper last night. You're a treasure, you know."

Miriam felt a surge of warmth. She knew, but only because Tilly had been telling her that all her life. "Thanks, Tilly. I love you. I hope you know that."

"I do, dear. I do. And I'd better check on Fred. He didn't sleep well last night."

Miriam watched her go, worry about Fred fighting with concern about her own travel plans.

She could wait.

Then Tilly returned, and the worry on her face gave Miriam pause. "I need to take him back to the hospital, and this time they're keeping him until they find out what's wrong. Do you mind staying a bit longer?"

"You're not taking him," Miriam protested. "You're way too tired. I'll take him in."

Tilly shook her head. "No. They always ask so many questions, and you can't answer them. And you have to get ready to leave. Besides, I don't want to put Taryn through a trip to town and back."

Miriam reluctantly agreed.

She helped Fred into the car, then watched as they drove away. Praying.

Now she was back at home, with nothing to do but wait for Jake. She had tried to text him to tell him about Simon's call, but it didn't go through. She suspected he was in a poor service area.

She went back into the house just as Taryn entered the kitchen, yawning and stretching. "I'm hungry."

A good sign. "I'm glad to hear that. What would you like for breakfast. Eggs and toast or cereal?"

"A muffin?"

Miriam was about to say no, but then figured there was no harm. So, she cut and buttered a muffin and poured a cup of orange juice for her.

"Where's Grandma and Grandpa?" she asked, breaking a piece off the muffin and eating it.

"Grandma had to bring Grandpa back to town. To see the doctor."

Miriam tried to keep the worry out of her voice, covering it with a smile.

"Okay." She sounded so matter of fact. "But now I need dessert."

"You don't have dessert for breakfast." Miriam cleared away her plate and cup.

"Can we have a marshmallow roast? My daddy always has one with me."

Miriam knew that to be a bit of an exaggeration but figured it was a perfect way to keep Taryn entertained for a while. She didn't know what else to do with the child, and it would probably be good for her to get outside.

Fifteen minutes later, they were squatting in front of a low-burning fire, toasting marshmallows. Taryn's face was smeared with the remnants of her most recent marshmallow, and Miriam regretted not bringing out a wet facecloth for her.

"You look grubby," Miriam said, reaching across to carefully wipe off the worst of it with the cuff of her shirt.

Taryn tried to cooperate by licking her chin with her tongue and wiping her face with her hand but only succeeded in making it worse. "I'm gonna need a bath," she said.

"Yes, you are." Miriam touched her nose lightly with her finger and smiled.

Taryn looked suddenly serious. "I heard Grandma say you're going away today. Why don't you want to stay?"

Miriam's heart sank at the sad look on the little girl's face and the plaintive note in her voice. She got up and, leading Taryn by the hand, walked over to the picnic table. They sat down together, and Miriam took a deep breath. "Remember the night I gave you a kiss on your hand?"

Taryn opened one sticky fist and looked down at it, nodding slowly, her ponytail bobbing.

"Well, that kiss was for when I'm going away." Miriam stopped as a lump in her throat cut off her speech. She waited a beat, then forced herself to continue. "I have to go back to work. I don't live here."

Taryn clenched her fist. "But I want you to stay." She looked up at Miriam, her soft brown eyes filling with tears. "Don't you want to stay with us? Daddy wants you to stay."

"I told you already, dear, I have to go back." Miriam stopped, then pulled Taryn against her, held her close.

Taryn wound her arms around Miriam in a tight hug. "But who is going to bring me to play school?" she cried, her voice muffled against Miriam's jacket.

"Your grandma will still be here. And your daddy."

Taryn sniffed loudly. "But Daddy has to work and Grandma has to take care of Grandpa. I want you to bring me."

Miriam pressed a kiss to Taryn's head, inhaling her scent. She felt a yearning toward her that she was sure had much to do with her own regrets, her own sorrow over lost opportunities.

She should have been mine, Miriam thought, closing her eyes. Remembering what Paula had written, she fought down a surge of anger, of hate over what her friend had done and the repercussions of it.

Once again, she struggled to forgive her mother for sending her away, for blackmailing Jake.

Am I never going to be done with this? she prayed, rocking Taryn lightly, the hurt magnifying the more she thought of her mother, of her friend. To forgive was difficult enough, but to forgive someone who wasn't even there seemed futile.

At the same time, Miriam knew that if she was going to go

back east stronger than when she'd arrived, this was precisely what she had to do. Forgive.

Please, Lord, help me to get through this. Help me to forgive them. I can't do any less because I know how much You forgave me. Miriam finally realized what she was saying in her own prayer. She *had* been forgiven. The guilt she felt over past sins, her feelings of shame, had all been forgiven, thoroughly and completely. Yet she still struggled to give that same forgiveness to her mother and her best friend.

Miriam took a slow breath, and another, and then gently set Taryn away from her. "Let's go in the house and get washed up, okay?" she said quietly, wiping away a tear from Taryn's cheek with her thumb.

Taryn sniffed, nodded once, and jumped off the picnic table. She stopped, her head cocked to one side. "Do you hear that?" she asked. "I hear Grandma's car." She grinned back at Miriam and ran toward the driveway.

But as they came around the house, the vehicle turning in wasn't Tilly's car but a silver sports utility vehicle, its shiny finish coated with a thin layer of dust.

The license plates told her that it was a rented vehicle. Simon most likely, she assumed as she glanced at her watch.

"Come back here, Taryn. Wait until he's turned off his vehicle," Miriam warned.

Taryn paused as the SUV parked beside Miriam's. Then as it came to a stop, she jumped up and down, clapping her hands. "It's Uncle Simon!" she shrieked.

A tall man got slowly out, stopped beside the vehicle, and stretched. He wore a leather jacket and blue jeans. His face was half covered with a pair of brown-tinted aviator glasses, and as he turned to look at Miriam, his mouth curved into a distinct smirk.

"Uncle Simon!" Taryn called out, running directly toward him.

"Hey, squirt," he said, bending over to grab the little girl.

"How's my favorite niece?" He swung her up in a hug, spun around, then set her down, holding her hand as he glanced over at Miriam. "Hey there." He slipped his glasses off his face and tucked them in the pocket of his coat. His smile grew broad and more sincere. He held out his free hand. "Look at you, all grown up and gorgeous."

Miriam remembered Simon as a much younger, lankier version of the man in front of her. He looked just like Jake, and yet not. But he had the same cocky smile and self-assured air.

"That happens," Miriam said quietly, returning his firm shake with an equally firm one. "And I'm sorry, but I haven't had time to run out to the field and tell Jake you were coming. I thought he'd be back by now, and I can't text him."

"Cell service in the country. Sub optimal," he said, adding a grin to his complaint. "Oh, well. I'll just wait."

"Do you want some coffee or tea?" she asked.

Simon grinned again. "Tea. That's what we drink in this house, isn't it, Taryn?" He swung her hand, grinning at her, then turned to Miriam. "So, we'll have a cup of tea, and then you can tell me all about what's happened in your life since the last time I saw you."

Miriam doubted that she would, so she just smiled and walked ahead of him into the house.

JAKE PULLED up the seed drill and glanced at the gathering clouds. Normally the thought of rain would have made him antsy, but thankfully he was done. The rain would be just perfect.

He drove the tractor to the road and got out to secure the drill for transport. Just as he was walking back to the tractor, the first few spatters of rain hit.

He had tried not to think about Miriam while he worked.

Had tried not to think of her leaving today. But he had spent most of the morning reliving what had happened yesterday. What could he have done different? How could he have convinced her to stay?

But she was adamant, and no matter what he had said, he couldn't break through the barriers she had erected. He knew she loved him. Was sure of it. She had said it herself. So, why did he have the feeling he was even worse off than before?

She was holding something back from him.

Was he going crazy all at once or if it had been coming on for some time?

He reached up and turned on the radio, hoping to find something other than the usual heartbreak and honky-tonk. He settled on a classical station, which soothed him.

By the time he returned home, he felt as if his emotions were finally under control—until he pulled into his driveway and, with a lift of his heart, saw Miriam's car was still here.

Right beside it was a rental vehicle. *Probably a salesman*, he thought, with a sigh of frustration. The last thing he wanted was to go over the merits of one kind of spray over another or what kind of baler he should buy. Not with Miriam still in his house and getting ready to leave.

Then he noticed that Tilly's car was gone, and fear gripped him. There was probably a simple explanation, but he was afraid.

He looked over the yard that his father had built up all these years. Other than his time with his first father, Tom Steele, Jake had spent some of his happiest years here.

He parked the tractor and the seed drill, giving himself a moment. Sending up a prayer for Fred. He felt emotionally vulnerable and drained. His father was ill, and he was in love with a girl who he knew wouldn't be satisfied living here. Not after the life she had lived. He had been utterly foolish to even entertain that idea.

He turned to trudge across the yard. The rain was coming down in earnest now, so he started to run.

As he opened the porch door, the sound of a man's deep laugh greeted him. Puzzled, he toed his boots off and set them aside, then walked into the kitchen.

A tall man sat with his back to Jake. Taryn, sitting on the chair nearby, chattered away to him. She was looking a lot better. The man turned as Jake entered the kitchen.

"Daddy, Uncle is here," Taryn called out as soon as she saw her father.

"Simon." Jake felt surprise as his brother stood up to greet him. "What in the world are you doing here?"

Simon grabbed Jake in a most unmanly hug, then pulled away, his expression serious.

"I took a chance," he said slowly, watching Jake's face intently. "I talked to Miriam this morning, right after I got a call from Jonathan. You remember him? The Mountie?"

Jake nodded. Jonathan had helped discover information that brought Simon and Jake together.

"You might want to sit a minute, and I'll tell you what I found out." Simon pulled out a chair and set it out for his brother. "It's about our mother."

Jake chanced a quick look at Miriam, who stood by the sink, watching him, her expression enigmatic.

He frowned as he realized something. "Where's Tilly and Fred?"

Miriam bit her lip, glancing from him to Simon. "Tilly just took Fred to the doctor. He wasn't feeling well."

"What? And you didn't call me."

"I tried, but there was no service."

He held up his hands in a placating gesture.

"Sorry. I shouldn't have snapped." Stress mixed with the emotions that Miriam created in him. Emotions he had to push down.

Because she was leaving.

"It's okay," she said, her voice quiet. "Fred is fine. Just a bit dehydrated so they started him on IV fluids. Tilly figures he'll be home tomorrow."

Relief and confusion vied with each other as he nodded.

Okay. One crisis averted.

He turned back to Simon, not really wanting to deal with whatever hare-brained scheme his brother was now presenting.

"So what do you have that's different from what we both already know."

"I discovered her last known address before she died."

"Why didn't you phone to tell me?"

"I didn't want to do that. After all these years, I'd just as soon go up, see if it's true, and if it is—" he shrugged "—we'll take it from there. It's the closest we've come since I started looking."

And it had been a long search for his brother, thought Jake, remembering the number of homes Simon had run away from partly in the hope he would find his mother and partly to attain his independence. The whole point of the search was to reunite the family—Jake, Simon, and their mother.

But Jake had found contentment and happiness with the Prins family and could not be convinced the last time Simon had wanted to run away.

So, Simon had left. It was only in the past half year that they had found each other again. But even now, Jake wasn't sure he wanted to spend the time and energy that Simon did in what seemed like a fruitless search.

And his timing was atrocious.

"She's gone, Simon. We need to accept that. And I can't go. Obviously, Fred isn't doing well. Tilly needs my help. I've got Taryn to think of…" Jake's voice trailed off as he glanced at Miriam, unable to voice the rest of his thoughts. *I need to talk to Miriam before she leaves again.* "It's ridiculous."

"What's ridiculous about it, Jake?" Simon leaned closer. "What's so hard about wanting to finally get closure to all of this?"

"I'm sorry, Simon," he added, dragging a hand over his face. "I'm tired. I've got a lot on my mind, and I just don't think I can do this right now. We don't even know if she'll be there when we get there. It will be just like the last time."

"Maybe. But I want to know."

Simon leaned back in his chair, his arms crossed over his broad chest. "I'm going, whether you're coming with me or not. I just thought it would be better if we both went."

Jake understood the wisdom of that and understood Simon's unspoken request for help and support. Simon never wanted to admit when he needed help. You just had to know.

And Jake knew. Right now, what Simon wanted, as much as to find their mother, was for Jake to come along with him.

"I'm sorry, Simon. I can't see my way around this. Besides, what if it's a dead end again? What if we find out she moved somewhere else? What if she's not even alive?"

"Don't say that," Simon snapped, suddenly angry.

Jake held his brother's narrowed eyes, determined not to back down. Simon had spent endless hours, days and weeks, years on this quest.

He was worried about his brother's obsession with it. While Jake had his own questions, he had learned to lay many of them to rest. He wasn't about to create this fairy-tale ending where they found out that their mother was a saint forced into a bad situation. He knew it could easily go the other way. A darker ending. She might easily be someone they might not want to get to know better.

"It's a possibility we have to think about."

"Maybe. But this time around, I have a name. Jocelyn. Jocelyn Andrews. And there's no other place that name shows up." Simon leaned forward, his expression full of entreaty. "Please. Let's at least check this out. If we find out she's gone,

maybe passed away, then at least we can lay that to rest…
correction, I can lay that to rest."

Jake sighed, his sympathy for his brother's quest battling
with the practicality of his situation.

"Sorry, Simon. Much as I'd like to support you, I'm on my
own here. Tilly, Fred, Taryn. I can't leave."

"I can stay, if that's the problem," Miriam spoke up.

Jake swung around. "What do you mean? I thought you
had to leave."

"I can put it off a few days."

Jake held her eyes with his, as if to delve into her mind,
trying to figure out what was going on. "Why would you do
that?"

Miriam didn't answer and instead turned to Simon. "Can
you take Taryn for a short walk outside, please?"

Simon looked at her and then nodded. "C'mon, squirt.
You have to show me your yard."

Taryn jumped off her chair, eager to go out with her
uncle.

They left, and Miriam sat at the table beside Jake.

"Now…what did you have to say that Taryn couldn't
hear?" Jake asked, trying to keep his voice even. As if her
mere presence didn't make his heart rate jump. Didn't create
this longing to reach out and touch her.

Miriam looked down at her hands, pressed her slender
fingers together. "I think you should go with Simon, Jake," she
said quietly. "I think it's important that you try to find out
what you can about your mother. That you and Simon do it
together. And, if she's not alive, you need to find some closure.
To know for sure."

Jake caught a whiff of her perfume, watched how the light
of the window lit up her hair, placed hollows in her cheeks
and the delicate bones of her shoulders. They were alone.
How was he supposed to listen to her telling him to leave?
How was he supposed to keep a clear head and have a sane

discussion about a mother he never knew and hadn't thought much about in the past sixteen years?

How was he supposed to do that when the woman he had been thinking of all those years now sat across from him, so close and yet so distant? All he wanted to do was pull her into his arms and kiss her until she agreed to stay.

But that's not what she wanted to talk about.

And he knew that was not how things would end for them.

He pulled his attention back to what she was saying. "Why do you want me to go?" he repeated.

"Because..." Miriam bit her lip. "I guess it's because I ignored my own mother's needs so long. I got caught up in the things I wanted to do. I hated her for so long for taking me away from you. I hated her because you got married. I still struggle with forgiving her." Miriam stopped, pressing her hand against her mouth, and looked away.

Jake fought a manly battle to resist pulling her to him; he could tell she wasn't done.

Miriam lowered her hand into her lap, scratched at the polish on her nails. "I haven't lived the best life since I started modeling. That was my own choice. No one forced me into that. I spent a lot of time taking very good care of myself and making sure I had fun. What you read in the papers wasn't entirely true, but it wasn't too far off the mark when it came to my selfishness. I hardly visited my mother, hardly spent time with her. I thought she had to be punished for what she had done to me."

Miriam paused again.

"Your mother was a difficult woman," Jake reminded her. "It wasn't all your fault."

Miriam smiled. "Thanks for that. But I never realized what I had been holding back. My mother became a Christian in the hospital. The past few months of her life, when I was struggling with trying to keep my business afloat, I used to visit her more often. She was hard to visit with—she talked so slow.

But she kept telling me that I had to lay my burdens on the Lord." Miriam laughed shortly, glancing up at Jake, then away. "It seemed too easy. I didn't think God could bail me out of my business troubles."

"What business troubles?" Jake was a little lost.

Miriam looked startled, as if surprised at what he said. Then she waved a hand between them and carried on. "Doesn't matter. Not important. What I wanted to tell you was that when my mother died, I still hadn't forgiven her." Miriam looked up at Jake, her eyes steady. "The other day, sitting under the maple tree in our old front yard, you showed me something. And I discovered a few things about myself. I found out that I had no right not to forgive my mother when God had forgiven me so much."

Jake wasn't sure what to say to that. So, he just kept quiet, listening, hoping, and waiting to hear what he too desperately wanted.

That she would stay here.

"I know I'm not done," she continued. "I know I have a long way to go. But what I wish more than ever is that I had spent more time with her. That I had taken the time to sit with her. To learn beside my mother's bed what I had to learn without her around." Miriam leaned closer, taking Jake's hand. "You have that chance. You have a chance to have some questions answered, to find out why she gave you up. I'm sure you must wonder, just as I wondered why my mother did what she did to me. I still don't think it was right, but I've had to accept that she did it because, in her own way, she cared."

Jake wanted to deny what she was saying. What his mother had done was selfish. Her threats had been cruel and frightening to a young boy who was so unsure of his own place in the family he had been placed in. But he knew he had to deal with this on his own.

Had things turned out differently between him and Miriam, he might have an easier time dealing with it. But

Miriam sat across from him now, urging him to leave, urging him to pursue a different part of his life even though he was sure she knew there was something building between them.

He clutched Miriam's delicate hand in his own and lifted it to his face, holding it against his rough cheek, as if seeking strength from her touch.

He felt her fingers curl against his cheek, and he turned, pressing a kiss to its soft palm, breathing out in a sigh of longing. And lingering behind that, hope, drawing him on across the emptiness of his life. Hope that when he came back, he could convince her, one more time, to stay.

"I'll stay and help Tilly and be here for her," Miriam said. "I know you're finished seeding. You shouldn't miss out on this chance. I don't think you should do this with a phone call—I think you need to do this face to face."

Jake stood facing her, his hands in his pockets. "Why do you want to do this for me?" he asked, still struggling to understand why she seemed so adamant. "I thought you had to go today."

"Don't worry about my life, Jake," she said. "It's not worth the effort." She looked up at him. "But you have a chance to find out more about your mother. Maybe it's a way of my own mother's death making sense…if someone besides me can learn something from it."

Jake understood her need. But it didn't seem to fit with what he wanted to do. He prayed they would find a time and place where they could finally speak the truth to each other. "Okay," he said quietly. "I'll go. As long as you will be here when I come back."

"I will." She relaxed back in her chair.

And that fragile hope strengthened.

"I'm pretty sure we won't be gone long. Probably two days at the most." This was not the conversation he had had in mind. He didn't quite know what he had expected. But for now, knowing she would be here when he returned was enough to cling to.

"Good," was all Miriam said. She got up, and for a heart-stopping moment, Jake thought she was going to come up to him, wrap those slender arms around him, pull his head down to hers...

He forced the thought aside as she walked past him to the porch. "Where are you going?" he asked, his voice brusque with repressed emotions.

Miriam turned to him, her eyes hopeful. "I'm just going to get—"

"Taryn wants a drink." Simon's loud voice interrupted. He knocked on the open screen door. "Can we come in now?"

Miriam looked away. "Sure. We're done."

"Good." The door creaked as Simon pulled it open, and Taryn was chattering about the calves as she came in. She bounced into the kitchen and ran straight to her father. "I need a drink, Daddy."

"What do you say?" Jake and Miriam spoke at precisely the same time. Their eyes caught and held, and Jake could see Miriam blush.

"Sorry," she murmured.

"Please can I have a drink," Taryn said with studied impatience. "Then I want to go outside again."

"I'll go with you, Taryn," Miriam offered. "I have to clean up the picnic stuff anyhow."

"Okeydokey," Taryn said, then noisily gulped down a cup of juice that Jake had poured for her. She wiped her mouth and ran outside again.

Jake watched them leave, feeling as if an opportunity had passed.

"So," Simon asked, leaning against the kitchen counter. "I'm leaving in about an hour. Are you coming?"

Jake glanced out the window at Taryn and Miriam, who were cleaning up around the fire pit. He could see Taryn was chattering excitedly to Miriam. She leaned toward her, and Miriam gave her a quick hug. Again, he was struck with a sense that this was how it should be. A family—

"Jake," Simon called out with a laugh. "I'm over here, not out there."

"Sorry." Jake averted his gaze and took a deep breath. "I've decided to come with you," he said.

Simon was quiet for a moment, as if acknowledging the difficulty of the decision. "I know this is a hard time for you to leave. But I'm scared if we wait any longer, we'll miss her. I am really praying that it will work out in the end."

"So am I," said Jake fervently, thinking not only of Fred and Tilly, but of Miriam, as well. "So am I."

"I'M glad Jake stopped by the hospital on his way out," Tilly said as she sat back in her recliner in the living room. "Otherwise, I wouldn't have known anything about him going."

"How do you feel about him doing this?" Miriam asked, curling up in one corner of the couch.

Tilly shrugged as she picked up a magazine. "I think it's a good idea. Jake has never said much about his biological mother, but I know, since he had Taryn, he's been curious. I know he's wondered what would make a woman give up two boys like she did. I imagine she must have been in quite a difficult position to do that."

"I pray he finds her," Miriam said simply.

"I'm glad you could stay awhile longer," Tilly said. "Otherwise, Jake couldn't have gone at all. This won't make your trip back too rushed?"

Miriam shrugged the comment away. Each minute she stayed here added driving time to the trip. It would be tense, but if Jake came back when he said he would, she could make it by driving and sleeping in her car. "I'll be okay."

"And when you do go back, we are going to hear from you again, aren't we? I don't want you to feel you're all alone."

"I'm not, Tilly. I know how wrong I was to stay out of touch…" Her voice trailed off as she thought of what she had deprived herself of—Fred and Tilly and the love they had for her.

"I care for you, girl, and I sense that you are uptight about this job you have to do. Do you want to talk about it?"

Miriam gently shook her head. "I can't. But I want you to know that I'm not going back because I want to. I have…obligations."

"Well, I want you to remember that you can always talk to the Lord." Tilly leaned over and pulled out her Bible. She leafed through it and glanced up at Miriam. "This is a piece I like to read when I worry about the future." She adjusted her glasses and began to read from Psalm 71. "In you, O Lord, I have taken refuge; let me never be put to shame. Rescue me and deliver me in your righteousness; turn your ear to me and save me."

Miriam listened to Tilly's soft voice, letting the words comfort her. Then Tilly read, "'Though you have made me see troubles, many and bitter, you will restore my life again; from the depths of the earth you will again bring me up. You will increase my honor and comfort me once again.'"

"Can you read that again?" Miriam asked, sitting up.

As she did, Miriam took a deep breath, as if to draw the very essence of the words into her. It was a promise. Did she dare cling to it? Did she dare think it would be true for her?

Tilly read on and Miriam listened, feeling strengthened and nurtured. Nothing had changed, but she felt as if she had been given a port in the storm. Somehow, she had to trust.

Chapter 13

"Let's stop here." Simon slowed down by the restaurant just off the main road going through town, then turned in and parked in an empty spot right beside the building. He turned off the engine and laid his head back, eyes closed. Neither he nor Jake said anything. They were tired and disheartened and, if Jake were honest, broken-hearted.

For a long time they both sat, each lost in their thoughts. Finally, Simon put his hand on Jake's shoulder but still looked ahead.

"I'm sorry," was all he could manage.

Jake felt another surge of sorrow, allowing himself a moment of wishing he hadn't come along with Simon.

But that was moot. Simon would have gone on this quest regardless. And he would have been on his own when he found out.

"At least we know. For sure." Jake covered Simon's hand with his own, gave it a quick squeeze, then lowered it. "And I'm glad I was with you. When we found out."

Simon swallowed and nodded, still looking sightlessly through the windshield of his car.

Despite his own reluctance to look for his mother, Jake was now grieving their loss.

To find out, after all their work and looking, that their mother had passed away.

In childbirth.

They'd had their answer but at the same time, it had created another question. Where was the child she gave up?

And did they want to go chasing that lead down?

"Let's go," Simon said, getting out.

Jake slowly followed suit, stiff after the miles of driving.

He wanted to stretch his legs. They'd spent the past two days driving, put on over a thousand miles, and talked to a dozen people. Knowing they still had another two hours ahead of them before they were home made him feel exhausted. He hadn't seen this much of Alberta since he and Simon were getting shuffled around the foster care system.

"How are you doing?" Simon asked, getting out of his side of the vehicle. "With all this?" He let the sentence drift off.

Jake gave into an impulse, walked over to his brother, and gave him a hug. They clung to each other for a long moment, united in a sorrow that was hard to articulate. Words never came easy for Simon, and Jake wasn't sure what to say.

He hadn't invested as much in the search as Simon had, but still, to find out after all this time, that she'd been gone the entire time Simon had been looking was devastating.

"Sorry I dragged you through all this." Simon pulled back, swallowing, but then blew out a breath. "It's hard, like I said before, but at the same time, I feel like I finished the job. It was surreal, standing by her grave. But also surreal knowing there's someone else out there. A sibling."

Jake ignored the latter part of the sentence. He knew his brother—the information about his mother giving birth had eased away some of the sting, but the way his brother's eyes lit up when they found out told him Simon wasn't quitting until this was done.

"I'm glad we got to spend some time together," Jake said, as they walked past the huge windows to the entrance of the café.

"A lot of time," Simon said dryly, as they stepped into the restaurant.

"Are you staying the night when we get to the farm?" Jake asked, settling into a chair behind a table. He didn't even bother consulting the menu tucked between the sugar container and the napkin holder. He just wanted a cup of coffee and a muffin.

"Probably. If that's okay with Tilly."

"It'll be fine, and you know it."

"Will it be fine with Miriam?" Simon asked with a knowing smirk.

Jake ignored him. He didn't want to talk about Miriam with Simon. He didn't dare spend too much time even thinking about her.

"I remember a little pep talk you gave me one time," Simon continued, clasping his hands and resting them on the table, leaning forward. "I remember your telling me not to underestimate what I had to offer Caitlin. I wonder if it isn't my turn."

"What do you mean?"

"Look, I know as the big brother, you're supposed to be the one who has his act together, and for most of your life, you have." Simon sat back as the server stopped at their table with a pot of coffee. After she'd filled their mugs and left to place their order, Simon poured sugar in his coffee and began to stir. "You've always been the one who knows where he's going."

"And your point is?"

"You don't want Miriam to go."

"I don't," Jake agreed, blowing lightly on the steam of his coffee. "I don't want her to go, but she has to. Or so she keeps saying."

"Have you asked her why?"

"I've tried to, but she puts me off, like she doesn't want to tell me." Jake shrugged and took a careful sip of the coffee. "She's hiding something, but I can't get it out of her."

"You kissed her yet?"

Jake tried not to react, but his neck grew warm. "Yes."

"Oh, goodness, my ever-cool brother is looking a little sheepish." Simon grinned. "And?"

"And I can't believe I'm having this conversation with you, Simon. You sound like a teenager."

Simon laughed. "Caitlin always says I never really experienced childhood—that's why I won't grow up. So? Spill."

Jake sighed, knowing his brother wasn't going to quit. "I love her, Simon. Okay? I heard you say those words about Caitlin, and I remember feeling smug that I got you to admit it. So, now I'm saying the same thing. I love her." He rubbed his eyebrow with his index finger and shrugged.

"And…"

"And nothing. She lives a glamorous life. She's used to flying all over the world and making money. You saw that fancy little car of hers. Can you imagine her living in Fred and Tilly's house, getting by on a farmer's income, shopping in a little Podunk town like Waylen?"

Simon frowned as if contemplating. "You know what, Jake? I can."

Jake snorted. "You've only seen her for an hour. How in the world can you make that kind of assessment?"

Simon sat back with a self-satisfied grin. "Because I've seen the way she looks at you, big brother. That's why."

Jake heard what Simon said, his heart quickening. He thought of what Miriam had said just before he left, when she was trying to talk him into going to find out what happened to his mother. How she had accepted what God had done for her. Why would she tell him that?

He clutched his coffee cup, hardly daring to imagine that it could be.

"I guess you've got things to talk to little Miriam about when you get home," Simon continued.

"I don't have much left to ask her. I've laid everything out."

"Did you propose?"

Jake shot him a frown. "I did. But I don't know if I want to put myself out on a limb like again."

Simon grew serious, leaning forward. "Brother, if you really love her and you really care about her, you'll go so far out on that limb, you'll be clinging to tiny branches."

Jake chuckled at the visual.

"I say propose again. Then if she turns you down and if your pride can get that far, ask her why. And ask her to tell you the truth. That you need to know so you can move on."

Jake heard Simon's comments but knew he had to filter them. Going full at Miriam might backfire on him.

And yet….

The server came with their muffins, and Jake, feeling suddenly benevolent, smiled his thanks. She paused, her brown eyes holding his, then smiled carefully back.

She set the muffins down in front of them before leaving.

Simon unwrapped his muffin, frowning down at it, his mind obviously elsewhere.

"Tell me, Simon, where is your brain going now?"

Simon broke off a piece of his muffin, ate it, taking his time answering.

"Well, I feel like one question got answered. Not the way we wanted, that's for sure, but now we have another dilemma. Do we carry on? Do we go looking for this sibling? Or do we simply drop it?"

"I wish I knew." Jake scratched his head, still working through what they heard. "That might be even more complicated. All we have is our mother's name."

Simon shrugged, tapping the side of his mug with his finger. "I could ask Jonathan, Caitlin's brother, to help. He could contact some of his fellow officers—they might find out something for us. I wouldn't know where to start looking for this unknown sibling." Simon sighed, and Jake knew how disappointed he was. He felt the same, though his emotions were mixed right now. On the one hand, finding out about his mother did, as Miriam had suggested, bring about some closure.

"Would this person even welcome getting two unknown brothers in their life?" Jake added.

"Who knows?" He took another bite of his muffin, then his eyes grew wide. He covered his mouth while he finished chewing, his head bobbing as if he couldn't wait to get the words out. He swallowed, then grinned. "Hey. I have an idea of how we could find our brother or sister."

Jake took a sip of his coffee, giving himself a moment, bracing himself, so to speak. He always knew Simon was irrepressible, he'd just forgotten how quickly his brother shifted gears.

"Tell me more." Jake returned Simon's smile, wondering what his brother was concocting.

"So, Caitlin was bugging me about these ancestry DNA tests. Her sister got one for her birthday a couple of weeks ago, and Caitlin said she should give me one. I laughed it off, but now I'm thinking, what if we do one of those? Maybe we'll get a hit on that? Find someone who is related."

"But that only works if the other person does it as well, right?"

"Yeah. It's a 50/50 chance, but that's better than the odds we're fighting now."

Jake nodded an acknowledgement of that. "Okay. I guess we could do that."

Simon stared at him, as if he didn't believe what Jake just said. "Just like that?"

"Yeah? We've got nothing to lose."

"Some saliva and a few dollars, apparently. I can take one for the team if that's all I have to do."

"Okay. Let's do it then. See what happens."

They were quiet a moment, each lost in his own thoughts. Jake wondering what might come of this. Allowing himself a moment of sorrow at the loss of a woman he knew for such a short period of time.

"I want to thank you for coming, Jake," Simon said finally. "It meant a lot to me."

Jake merely nodded his acknowledgment. All the way to Riverview, he had doubted and wondered if he had done the right thing by going on this quixotic mission. But seeing the gratitude on his brother's face balanced out the frustration. Somewhat.

"More coffee, sirs?" Their server stopped by their table, holding a coffeepot in one hand.

"No, thanks. We've got a long ride ahead."

"Well, have a safe trip."

They walked out of the restaurant and into the warmth of the day, both anxious to get on their way.

The trip back to Waylen was quiet. Jake and Simon were each lost in their thoughts. The closer they got to home, the more uptight Jake got. Despite his brother's assurances about Miriam, Jake knew that there was a lot that couldn't be willed away. She had other obligations and was used to a life-style he couldn't begin to understand. And she had a secret she wasn't telling him.

As they pulled into the driveway, Jake sat straighter, looking for Miriam's car. He felt a clench of disappointment when he saw an empty spot where it had been two days ago.

"Looks like we're too late. Again," Simon said quietly.

"She might just be back at her house," Jake said, getting out of the vehicle. He almost ran to the house, anxious to find out where Miriam was.

Tilly sat in her usual chair in the living room when Jake burst into the room.

"Well, hello, Jake," she said, setting aside the book she was reading. "So glad you're home. And right on time like you said." She got up, carefully watching his face, probably to see if she could find any hint of what had happened. "So, how did it go? You didn't say much when you phoned to tell me when you were going to be home."

"We didn't find her." He wasn't about to blurt out the truth. Not like this.

"Oh, Jake." Tilly reached out for him and drew him into her arms. For a moment, Jake allowed himself the comfort, feeling a little guilty that his mind was on other things—on Miriam, rather than on the disappointment of finding out what happened to their biological mother.

Tilly pulled back, shaking her head. "That is too bad. Did you find out anything?"

Again, Jake weighed what to tell her. Later, he could fill her in.

"We found out she was pregnant before…" Jake smiled at his mother and shook his head, still unable to absorb that piece of news. "So, there might be a sibling out there."

"My goodness. That's interesting." Tilly clucked in sympathy.

"How's Dad?"

"He's much better. He's coming home tomorrow. It was just a flu he couldn't get over."

Tilly was about to ask something else, but after finding out that his father was going to be okay, Jake was done with amenities.

"Where's Miriam?"

Tilly pressed her hand to her cheek and sighed. "She's gone to her house. She got a phone call from some man named Carl. He called a couple of times. Once she knew when you were coming back, she made arrangements. She's only been gone a couple of minutes. I was supposed to give you a message. It's on the kitchen table."

Jake's heart plunged into his stomach. *A goodbye note,* he thought. This time, it was her turn. She had said she'd wait until he came back. Leaving just minutes before his return was cowardice. Miriam was avoiding him. And he was tired of it.

He ran into the kitchen, almost knocking Simon over in the process.

"What's up, Jake?"

"I don't know."

Jake bit his lip, almost swaying with weariness. If only he and Simon hadn't stopped at that restaurant. If only they had driven straight through. If only he hadn't gone with Simon in the first place.

If, if, if.

It seemed his entire life was punctuated with those words.

But he was tired of ifs. He wanted answers, and this time, he wasn't letting her go without finding them.

"Simon, I want you to take that my truck and park it across the main road. Miriam has to come by there on her way out. I don't want her leaving."

"Ah. A kidnapping."

"It's not that. Stop being so dramatic."

"I'm not the one running around shouting out random strange directions."

"Parking that vehicle right now would be good," Jake returned.

"Sure thing." Simon threw him a mock salute and jogged out the door.

Jake felt a measure of relief when he heard his truck start up. *First line of defense in place,* he thought. He turned to his mother, who handed him the folded note. "Did she say anything to you? Give you any hint why she decided to leave so suddenly?"

"Not really. Miriam had gone for a walk, and this Carl

fellow phoned. He asked where Miriam was. Said he couldn't get hold of her. I told him she was outside. Then he got angry and said something about her potentially blowing everything up. I asked him to explain." Tilly looked up at him, touching his shoulder lightly. "Jake, she risked losing an important job just to stay here. To help us out. Now she has to drive day and night to get there on time." Tilly shook her head. "It's a six-day drive to New York, and she has only four days to get there. It's too dangerous. Don't let her go."

Jake heard his mother's words, trying to understand, realizing that Miriam had made a huge sacrifice so he could try to find his mother. He also realized that she wasn't leaving until she gave him the reason why.

Jake's chest lifted in a sigh. "I'm going to her house."

Tilly gave him a hug. "I'll be praying for you both, son," she said, sniffing lightly.

Jake drew back, looked down at her softly wrinkled face, her bright blue eyes that shone with tears.

Son. He had lost his biological mother, but he had a true mother in Tilly.

Now all he had to do was find the other woman in his life.

He ran out to his truck which was still blocking the road. Simon was leaning against it, arms crossed, looking like a modern-day highwayman. "So far so good, brother," he said, as Jake came running up to him. "Don't come back without her," Simon warned.

"I won't." He jumped in, gunned the engine, spun around, and headed toward Miriam's place.

MIRIAM DROPPED the last of her clothes into the suitcase and zipped it shut. She couldn't help a quick glance at her watch, fear gripping her. Could she make it? Had she cut things too close? She pressed her hand against her stomach.

She wished she could have flown, but the ticket would have drained what little savings she had. Plus, she needed her car once she was back in New York.

It was going to be long hard drive. She would have to grab some sleep when possible.

She drew in another breath, wishing she had the nerve to stay and talk to Jake. But if she had, she might not have left. If she didn't do this job and the next and the next, her debt would keep building.

She had no choice.

Miriam thought of what Tilly had read to her while Jake was gone.

She walked out of the house and, without a second glance behind her, closed the door. The moon was out, and in its watery light, she could see the maple tree. She set her suitcase down and walked over to it, touched it. While it wasn't difficult to say goodbye to the house, it was going to be hard to leave this tree. For it was here that she had first felt the healing power of forgiveness.

She wondered if Jake could eventually forgive her.

She knew writing him a note was a cowardly move. It couldn't begin to cover what she felt. She didn't even know what she dared tell him. It was as if she were sixteen all over again, head over heels in love with Jake and unsure of herself.

A cool spring breeze danced around her, and she shivered a moment, thinking of the dear people she would be leaving behind here. She leaned against the tree, sending out prayers. She prayed Fred's health would improve. She prayed Tilly would be able to cope with it, knowing the deep love they had for each other. She prayed Taryn would get over her leaving. When Miriam had kissed the precious child good-night and told her she was leaving, Taryn had clung to her, crying and begging her to stay.

And then she thought of Jake. She didn't know how she could leave him again.

But she knew she had no choice.

She heard the sound of a truck engine, saw the lights sweep across the field as it turned into the driveway, then bob and weave as the vehicle came tearing down the lane, spewing gravel behind.

She straightened, then felt her mouth go dry as she recognized the truck that rocked to a halt, inches away from the back bumper of her car.

Her suitcase fell to the ground, her numb fingers unable to hold it, as Jake Steele flung the door of his truck open and strode toward her.

"Where are you going?" he demanded.

Miriam swallowed and took a step back. He was angry. She hadn't expected that.

She wanted to deflect his anger. "Did you find your mother?"

"I don't want to talk about my mother. Right now, it's more important to me to find out why you keep saying you have to go without telling me exactly why. I know modeling isn't that important to you, Miriam. You said you came here to finish things off. Your farm isn't sold, and I know that you still love me. I would say there are a few unfinished things to go yet."

Miriam leaned back against the tree, watching him in the pale moonlight, unable to speak.

"Miriam…" His voice softened and he paused and took a step closer. "I'm sorry. I shouldn't have been so angry. It's just…I'm frustrated…and afraid…I've told you once before, and I'm going to tell you again. I love you dearly. I love you more than I've ever loved anyone."

His words laid aside all the defenses she thought she had built against him. Flimsy barriers, indeed. And for a bright moment, she felt as if nothing was insurmountable.

"I want to take care of you. I want you to trust me. I want your problems to be my problems. I want you for better or worse, richer or poor—" he continued, his deep voice softly caressing.

"You don't know what you're taking on," Miriam said with a shaky cry. Once again, the burden of her debt dragged her down to earth, buried her hope.

"Then tell me. Tell me exactly what I'm taking on."

Miriam looked at him, heard the pain in his voice. He loved her. But could she and Jake find a way around what loomed over her? Would his love withstand it? There was only one way to find out.

"I'm in debt for eight hundred thousand dollars. Give or take a few hundred." The figure, spoken aloud, sounded even larger, even more insurmountable. "I need to sell the farm at a premium price, and I need to work to pay it down. I need to take on any job I can."

Jake's silence said more than any words he could have spoken. She wanted to curl up into a ball of misery; she wanted to let her sorrow overwhelm her.

She pressed her fingers against her mouth as if to hold back her cries. Her eyes were firmly shut. She had watched him leave once, and she couldn't do it again.

"Not going to lie, that's a lot of money…"

"It is," was all she could say. She turned away because she didn't want to see him walk away.

Then warm, hard hands turned her around, gently pulled her fingers away from her mouth.

"Doesn't change anything for me," he said quietly.

"What do you mean?"

"You're still Miriam. Still the girl who has captured my heart. Still the girl I'll always love."

She could only stare at him, trying to let what he was saying settle into her mind.

"But…it's so much money."

"Yes. But it's just money."

She hadn't heard that in ages. Not since she left the farm. Fred always said that.

Then she felt his soft, inviting lips on hers. Slowly, gently, Jake pulled her into his arms, one hand curling around her neck, the other clutching her waist. Distracting and compelling.

"Why didn't you tell me?" his soft voice feathered over her mouth, then he drew back to slip his fingers through her hair. Still here. Still with her.

"Because I was too ashamed. I trusted...trusted the wrong person. I let greed cloud my thoughts. I wanted what he was offering." She tucked her chin against her chest, still struggling to reconcile the girl she was then with who she had become. "I got pulled into a bad business decision all because I thought I could get more than what I had. Instead, I ended up with less than less." She stopped there, wondering if she should tell him everything, then figured, why not. What was one more humiliation? "The worst of it all was that the company that reneged on delivery was on the verge of bankruptcy. And, even worse, the owner of that company was a woman who Lance, my ex-boyfriend, was cheating on me with." She released a harsh laugh. "So sordid, cheap, and humiliating."

"You don't need to take on his horrible behavior. Bring it into who you are."

"No. But I trusted him. Dated him, in fact."

Jake was silent a moment. "I wouldn't put too much on your own shoulders. None of us here can say they haven't made mistakes."

Miriam wondered if he was talking about him and Paula.

"As for your business troubles, we can hammer out all the details later. I'm sure Simon would love to give you advice."

"There is no later. I have to leave now. In fact, I should have been on the road a day ago." She stared up into his loving eyes, still trying to absorb what he had just said.

"I know. And I can't tell you enough how much I appreciate your sticking around so I could go." He released a harsh laugh. "Even though it was a futile trip."

"No. What do you mean? What happened?"

Jake brushed his finger over her lips. "Again, a conversation for another time. Right now, we need to solve the problem that's right in front of us. You said you need to get to New York, and you were going to drive."

More shame slithered through her. "Yes. I...can't really afford a plane ticket."

"Okay. I can spot you that. Which gives us some breathing space."

His eyes held hers, soft, gentle, and in their chocolate depths, she saw no condemnation.

Only love.

"Please. Let me do that for you. For us."

Miriam felt a melting begin deep within her, a softening. She slipped her arms around him, her eyes still shut tight, as if she were afraid to open them to reality.

Jake's mouth moved slowly, gently over hers, and then, as her arms tightened, with more urgency.

Miriam felt the warmth of his mouth, hard on hers, his arms holding her tightly against his chest. She kissed him back, unable to hold him close enough, unable to show him adequately what she was feeling.

He murmured her name against her mouth and kissed her over and over again, his hands caressing her back, her head, his fingers tangling in her hair.

Finally, he drew away, but only to cradle her head against his, to hold her close to his pounding heart.

Miriam tried to absorb the onslaught of her own emotions as she leaned against his strength, her cheek pressed against his shirt, her arms holding him, his chin caressing her head again and again.

"Don't go, Miriam," he pleaded. "Please don't leave me again. I don't think I can go through this a second time."

She felt his chest lift in a huge, shuddering sigh. "I don't care about the money, about your debt. We can figure this out. It's not too much to pay for having you with me. Nothing is."

Miriam closed her eyes, resting in this momentary haven, letting his words pull her along, beguile and captivate her. She had to trust him, had to believe him. Because if she didn't, what in life was there for her?

She lifted her face to look at him, and in the light of his truck's headlights she saw tears on his cheeks. With a trembling finger, she touched them, awestruck at the sight, at the evidence of the depth of his feelings for her.

As she traced the path of his tears, she whispered his name, her own throat thickened with emotion. "I love you, too, Jake." She stopped, her voice breaking. Then the words came pouring out of her. "I don't think I ever stopped. I've never stopped thinking of you, wondering how you were, not daring to call because then I would hear your voice and start missing you all over again." She took a quavering breath. "It hurt so much to miss you. I didn't think I could go on. And now, to know that you still love me despite...despite everything..." She couldn't continue. Laying her head against his chest, she fought for control.

"Miriam, I have prayed to hear you say that." He laid his damp cheek on her head. "Say it again," he whispered.

"I love you." The words were muffled, but strong. Then she looked up at him again, her hands cradling his beloved face. "I love you, Jake Steele."

"Enough to marry me?"

His words were the second, maybe the third shock she had to endure.

"Marry you?"

"Yes. Like with a ceremony and a ring and a dress and whatever you want."

"And Taryn?"

His mouth curved into that familiar, heart quaking smile, a gift she was allowed to take freely.

"Taryn loves you already. I'm not worried about how it will all work. I know there'll be challenges. I'd be a fool if I thought we will have smooth sailing, but I can't imagine going on and doing life without you around again. Please say yes."

"You don't need to ask me twice," she said, slipping her arms around his neck, meeting his hungry mouth, tasting, caressing. Letting the cares of the moment slip away.

For now.

He lifted his head and feathered a light kiss over her mouth, his gaze full of wonder, his fingers caressing her neck. "Oh, Miriam, I hardly dared hope. God has been so good."

Miriam reached up to touch his hair, her fingers reveling in its thickness. "You might not think so once you talk to your banker."

He shook his head. "Again. A conversation for later."

"But it's so much money," she couldn't help but repeat. "You couldn't afford to buy my land. How—?"

The rest of her words were cut off by his mouth covering hers. When he finally pulled away, he touched her lips with his finger. "I said I don't want to hear about it. Not yet. Let's just celebrate this moment. I'm not worried."

She let her head drop against his chest as he lowered his hand. "I love you so much," she whispered. "I can't believe you're willing to take this on."

"Because we're doing it together, that makes it much easier. A burden shared is a burden halved. You're not alone anymore."

As Miriam leaned against his chest, she let her prayer of thankfulness drift up to heaven. She had come here to rest, to recoup—and then go back to the drudgery of her work. Still struggling. Still alone.

But God had had other things in mind for her.

"Let's go home, Miriam," Jake murmured, giving her

another tight hug. "There are a few people who want to know what's happening."

She caught him by the arm. "Jake," she said quietly. "You need to know I don't want to do the job, but it will pay me a lot of money. And if I don't do it, I stand to lose other jobs."

"Like I said, we'll buy a plane ticket. That still gives you a couple of days here."

Miriam felt as if a huge weight had fallen off her shoulders. "It might work out. Maybe."

Jake gave her a little shake. "You're not alone in trying to figure this out, Miriam. Not anymore."

He bent over to take her suitcase, and then, his arm around her, hers wrapped around him, as if they were afraid to let each other go, they walked to his truck. Jake tossed her suitcase in the back and helped her in, then pulled her against him as, one-handed, he spun the steering wheel around and headed home.

Then he took off down the driveway, barely slowing for the turn off onto the road and then taking off. He pulled to a halt at his own place, held her close a moment.

"I love you. I love you," he whispered, kissing her once again.

"I'm nervous, you know," she confessed.

"About what?"

"Taryn, Tilly. Will I be able to do it?"

"You know, Miriam, I think, deep down, you're not a model. I think you're a mother at heart."

His words comforted her, and together they walked up the sidewalk. Together they stepped into the house.

Taryn looked up from the kitchen table, blinked, then grinned as she saw Jake and Miriam.

"Daddy, Miriam," she yelled, running and throwing herself at both of them. Jake caught her, Miriam caught an arm, and the three of them held each other as Miriam's tears flowed freely.

"Let me guess—you talked her into staying," Simon drawled, turning around in his chair. He got up, shook Jake's hand, and gave Miriam an awkward hug. Taryn got in the way, squealing with delight.

Tilly came into the kitchen to see what the commotion was about and smiled broadly. "My goodness," she said, pressing a hand to her mouth. She, too, joined in the celebration.

They explained to Taryn what was to happen, and the child immediately began hugging and kissing Jake and Miriam indiscriminately.

Later, when Taryn was finally down for the night and Simon and Tilly had gone to bed, Miriam and Jake had some time to themselves again. They sat on the couch, Jake's arms firmly around Miriam as if he didn't dare let her go.

He had told her about his mother. About a potential sibling. Simon had said to let it go. He was taking care of figuring this out.

And though Miriam was sad for Jake, he hadn't stopped smiling since they came back from her farm.

Miriam traced circles on the soft hair of his forearm, bemused at the difference ten years had made in this man she loved so dearly. "Jake," she asked quietly.

"Miriam," he replied, his voice teasing.

"I am serious." She hesitated, but she needed one more reassurance. "I need to know, Jake—are you sure you know what you're getting into?"

Jake sighed, his breath gentle across her head. "Miriam, I'm not worried. It's only money."

"But it's so much."

"It is. I won't deny it. But if you sold that land to someone else, I would have lost it anyway. I've been thinking I could sell one of the other quarters of land, by Rock Lake. Then I'd buy yours from you." He laid his cheek on her head. "The rest of the debt, we'll have to work into the farm debt. Prices are good. We'll figure it out." He hugged her again. "I told you already, I'll do anything to have you stay with me."

Miriam bit back her next protest and relaxed against Jake, reveling in his strength, in the ability to lean on someone for the first time in years. It still felt strange—wrong almost—yet liberating to put all her fears and worries into someone else's hands.

Jake nuzzled her head. "Have I told you I love you?"

"Not for about two minutes." Miriam turned her face up to him, and Jake kissed her.

"I used to dream of sitting with you on this couch," Jake said softly, tracing the line of her eyebrow, the curve of her cheek, the line of her lips.

"I did, too. I used to dream we could walk down Main Street holding hands, just like all the other lovers do."

"Well, it's taken a few years, but we can."

Then on that same couch, Miriam kissed her future husband.

And sent up a prayer of thanks. Their lives had taken some twists and turns to arrive at this destination, but they were finally here.

Together, at last.

Epilogue

"*N*ow stay close to me. It's really busy here," Jake said to Taryn as they made their way through the throng of people in the airport. She clung to his hand.

Jake had wanted to carry her, but according to her, a big girl didn't need to be carried.

From speakers overhead, a voice announced the arrival of yet another flight as Jake worked his way to the arrival gate.

People wearing trench coats and suits mingled with individuals in blue jeans, sweatsuits, and leather jackets for a spot close to the gate where the passengers from flight number 264 direct from New York were to arrive.

"Is she coming yet?" Taryn asked, clutching the bouquet of flowers Jake had picked up before coming here. "I don't want the flowers to die."

"They won't," Jake assured his daughter. "They'll still be fresh and pretty when you give them to her."

Taryn looked up at him, smiling widely. "When I get big, I want to fly on a plane, just like Mims gets to."

"That would be fun, wouldn't it?"

Taryn nodded, then buried her nose in the flowers, taking a deep sniff.

A burst of noise came from the arrival doors, and Jake looked up, his expectations making his heart skip. She was coming. After a two-week absence, Miriam was coming home.

The doors swung open again and there, behind a group of laughing young kids, he saw her.

She wore a loose apricot-colored crop top over cargo pants. Casual clothing, yet Miriam managed to lend an aura of elegance and style to the simple lines.

Her hair shone under the bright lights, wisps of it accenting her face, her eyes scanning the crowd as eagerly as Jake watched her.

She hadn't seen him yet, he realized as she paused, frowning lightly, clutching the large, oversize bag she always carried with her as hand luggage.

He noticed a few men glance her way then stop, their faces showing their obvious admiration. One man elbowed his neighbor who looked her way, then also stared.

For a moment, Jake resented their gaping, but Miriam was unaware of the minor sensation she was causing.

She stood up on tiptoe, scanning the crowd, frowning.

Then, the frown melted, her eyes widened, and she began to run.

"Jake," she called out, totally unselfconscious about her reaction.

Jake's heart quickened at the sight of her rushing toward him, her arms wide, laughing.

"You're here," she said.

He let go of Taryn's hand for an instant and caught her as Miriam flung her arms around him. He swung her up, holding her close, his head buried against her soft neck.

"Oh, Miriam," he murmured, "I missed you, I missed you."

They held each other a moment, yet unable to hold each other close enough, hard enough.

He pulled back and gently lowered her to the ground.

They gazed lovingly at each other, then he lowered his head and with reverence kissed her mouth.

"How are you?" he asked, drawing slightly back, as he noted each dear feature, as if looking for any changes in her.

"Better. Now." She reached up and stroked his hair back from his face. "Much better." Then, she turned to Taryn. "Hi, sweetheart." She dropped to one knee and hugged her tightly. "I missed you, little Pip."

"I missed you, too, Mims." Taryn held out the flowers. "We got these for you."

Miriam took the flowers, sniffed them appreciatively, and grinned at Taryn. "They're beautiful. We'll have to put them in water when we get home, won't we?"

Taryn nodded, then took Miriam's hand. "Daddy can take your bag," she said imperiously.

"Yes, ma'am." Jake saluted, bent over, and slung the bag over his shoulder. As he straightened, he noticed a few puzzled glances from the men who had been ogling Miriam, as if they were wondering how some rough looking farmer wearing blue jeans, a twill shirt, and a cowboy hat managed to snag this exotic-looking woman.

"What's the matter, Jake?" Miriam asked, as she stood, holding Taryn's hand, her flowers clutched in the other.

"I'm still trying to get used to having all these guys staring at my wife."

Miriam frowned, then looked back over her shoulder in the direction Jake was glowering. "What guys?" she asked.

The men who had been looking quickly averted their curious gazes.

"Oh, those guys," Miriam said, glancing back at Jake with a shrug. "It doesn't mean anything."

"Maybe not. But I don't like it."

Miriam leaned against him, smiling coyly up at him. "But I'm not looking, am I?"

"I hope not."

Miriam's expression grew serious. "Jake, I would love nothing more than to stay here every day. To be wearing dirty blue jeans and a shirt smeared with flour. You know that."

Jake grinned down at her, his heart overflowing with love for the beautiful woman. "I know that. And only two more jobs and you'll be done."

Miriam sighed and nodded her head in affirmation. "Hallelujah. Goodbye to jet lag, to tight clothes, cranky photographers, and temperamental clients."

"We did it, you know," he said as he slipped his arm around her. They began walking toward the exit. "It's just about done, that insurmountable debt you couldn't tell me about."

"Well, I'm really glad Simon was the one who bought the land. That way, I can say I still own my old house," Miriam said, smiling lightly.

"Maybe someday we'll be able to buy it back, but for now, I'm happy enough to rent it from him."

The automatic doors slid open at their approach, and Jake had to stop Taryn from wanting to go through them again.

"Miriam wants to go home," he said to her as they walked across the taxi lane toward the parking garage.

Taryn skipped beside them, still holding Miriam's hand. "I have a friend in grade one," she announced to Miriam. "She has a mommy and a daddy too." Taryn looked up at Miriam, a slight frown creasing her forehead. "But she doesn't call her mommy, Mims. You and Daddy said I didn't have to call you Mommy, but can I? Please?"

"Oh, sweetheart." Miriam stopped and, bending over, pulled Taryn into her arms. "Of course you can."

Jake watched the two of them, both beautiful, both so very precious to him, and felt a fullness wash over him at what Taryn had just asked.

Miriam stood and as she turned to Jake, he saw her wipe

her eyes. She bit her lip and glanced up at him. "Does it get any better than this?" she asked, reaching out to him as well.

"I doubt it," he said, pulling her close. He caught Taryn in a hug, lifted her up, and with one arm, held her as well.

He and Miriam exchanged another quick kiss and then, arm in arm, they walked down the ramp toward Jake's truck.

A father. A daughter. A mother.

And a love as precious and dear as a cowboy's smile.

I'M sure you're curious about the rest of Jake and Simon's story. If you want to find out more, you can find out by clicking on the cover for the next book in the series, Love like a Slow Country Song.

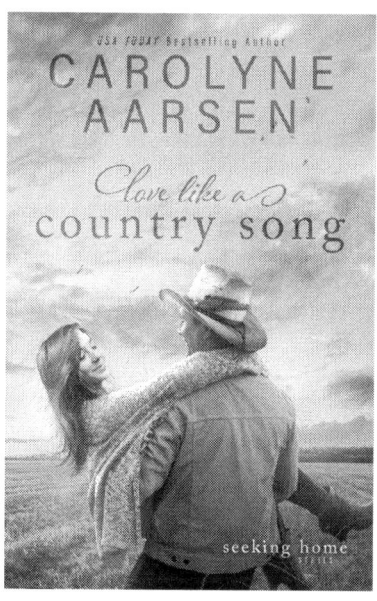

THANKS FOR READING SO FAR! If you want to find out more about me and stay abreast of all my new releases you can sign up for my newsletter by clicking either on the book or on the words. When you do, you'll be receiving a free book from me.

SIGN UP FOR MY READER GROUP

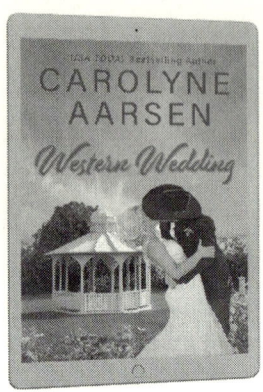

TAKE care and blessings to you on your own journey of life.

Carolyne
www.carolyneaarsen.com

About the Author

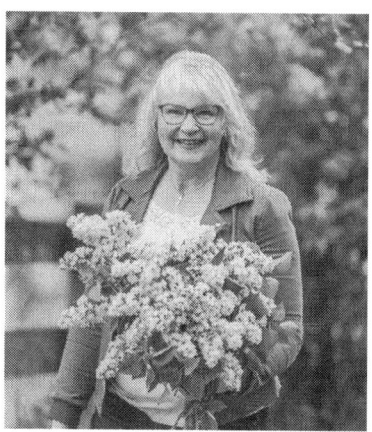

My husband and I live on a small ranch in Northern Alberta, where we have raised four children and numerous foster children, and are still raising cattle and trying to keep two dogs under control. When the grandkids come, everything gets dropped to spend time with them.

I craft my stories in my beautiful office with a large west-facing window, through which I can watch the changing seasons while struggling to make my words obey. Sometimes they do, sometimes they don't. Even after all the words I've put down the perfect story has still eluded me.

Someday.

Meantime you can find out more about me by visiting my website - www.carolyneaarsen.com

Thanks for reading my books. Without you, there would be no reason to sit at my computer each day.

Made in the USA
Middletown, DE
29 December 2023